GREETINGS FROM SOMEWHERE

BY HARPER PARIS • ILLUSTRATED BY MARCOS CALO

LITTLE SIMON

New York   London   Toronto   Sydney   New Delhi

This book is a work of fiction. Any references to historical events, real people, or real places are used fictitiously. Other names, characters, places, and events are products of the author's imagination, and any resemblance to actual events or places or persons, living or dead, is entirely coincidental.

LITTLE SIMON

An imprint of Simon & Schuster Children's Publishing Division • 1230 Avenue of the Americas, New York, New York 10020 • This Little Simon hardcover edition May 2016 • Copyright © 2014 by Simon & Schuster, Inc. All rights reserved, including the right of reproduction in whole or in part in any form. LITTLE SIMON is a registered trademark of Simon & Schuster, Inc., and associated colophon is a trademark of Simon & Schuster, Inc. For information about special discounts for bulk purchases, please contact Simon & Schuster Special Sales at 1-866-506-1949 or business@simonandschuster.com.

The Simon & Schuster Speakers Bureau can bring authors to your live event. For more information or to book an event contact the Simon & Schuster Speakers Bureau at 1-866-248-3049 or visit our website at www.simonspeakers.com.

Designed by John Daly.

The text of this book was set in ITC Stone Informal.

Manufactured in the United States of America 0416 FFG

10 9 8 7 6 5 4 3 2 1

Library of Congress Control Number 2016932804

ISBN 978-1-4814-8510-4

ISBN 978-1-4424-9720-7 (*The Mystery of the Gold Coin* eBook)

ISBN 978-1-4424-9723-8 (*The Mystery of the Mosaic* eBook)

ISBN 978-1-4814-0298-9 (*The Mystery of the Stolen Painting* eBook)

ISBN 978-1-4814-0301-6 (*The Mystery in the Forbidden City* eBook)

These titles were previously published individually in hardcover and paperback by Little Simon.

TABLE OF CONTENTS

GREETINGS FROM SOMEWHERE

The Mystery of the Gold Coin

#1

TABLE OF CONTENTS

CHAPTER 1

The Surprise

"So what's the surprise?" Ethan Briar asked.

"Yeah, what is it, Mom and Dad?" Ethan's twin sister, Ella, chimed in.

Their mother, Josephine, smiled nervously. Their father, Andy, reached over and squeezed her hand. Ella tried to guess what they were going to say. Was it going to be a new puppy? Or maybe cool matching bikes?

"Ta-da! We're moving," Mr. Briar announced.

"You mean to a new house?" Ella asked, confused.

Mrs. Briar shook her head. "No, not to a new house. I just accepted a new job. I'm going to be the travel writer for the *Brookeston Times*."

"So why do we have to move? The *Brookeston Times* is in Brookeston," Ella pointed out. The *Times* was their town's newspaper—everyone read it.

"That's the exciting part," Mr. Briar said. "Starting next week we'll be traveling to different foreign cities so your mom can write about them."

"Foreign, like, another country?" Ethan asked.

"Yes," Mr. Briar said happily. "Like Spain and England

and Peru and India and—"

"Wait! Did you say *next week*?" Ella interrupted.

"Yep. We're leaving next Sunday," Mrs. Briar said.

"*Next Sunday?!*" Ethan exclaimed. "What about school? And soccer?"

"And our friends? And Grandpa Harry? Will we be able to visit them?" Ella asked.

"Well . . . ," Mrs. Briar paused. "Not right away. But we can stay in touch

with everyone. And, of course, we'll come back to Brookeston—"

"Someday. We're just not yet sure when," Mr. Briar finished.

Silence.

Ethan put his fork down. Ella had lost her appetite, too.

"It'll be the adventure of a lifetime," Mr. Briar said brightly. "We'll see some of the most incredible sights in the world! Places like the Great Wall of China, the Eiffel Tower in France—"

"Do they have soccer in China and France?" Ethan cut in.

"Yes, of course! And as for school, we've already spoken to Principal McDermott. I'll be homeschooling you both," Mr. Briar went on.

Mr. Briar was a history professor at Brookeston University. He was supersmart. He knew stuff like who invented the boogie board (Tom Morey) and the name of the first king of England (Egbert).

Still, Ella could not imagine their

dad being *their* teacher. He didn't sing silly "good morning" songs like their *real* second-grade teacher, Mrs. Applebaum. And he didn't serve green milk on St. Patrick's Day, either.

Mrs. Briar stood up. "Who wants dessert? Your dad picked up something special from Petunia Bakery to celebrate."

"I'm not hungry," Ella said quietly.

"Me neither. Can we go to the tree house?" Ethan asked.

Mrs. Briar cast a worried look at her husband. Ella and Ethan never turned down a treat from their very favorite bakery.

"Sure. We can just save you some dessert," Mr. Briar told them.

Ethan and Ella jumped up from the table and rushed out of the dining room.

Dessert was the last thing on their minds.

CHAPTER 2
Was It All a Dream?

The twins crossed the backyard to the old maple tree. The sky was deep blue with a sprinkling of stars. Crickets croaked in the distance. The air was cool and smelled like flowers.

They climbed the rope ladder up to the wooden tree house. Then they plopped down on the floor pillows.

"Worst. News. Ever," Ella declared.

"I don't get it. Mom already *has* a job with the *Brookeston Times*," Ethan said.

"This is a *different* job, though. She'll get to travel, just like Grandpa Harry did," Ella pointed out.

Grandpa Harry was their mom's dad. He was a famous archaeologist. That meant that he studied people from the ancient past by looking at buildings, artwork, and other things they left behind. When his wife, Grandma Lucy, was still alive, they used to travel all over the world for his work.

"Where are we going to live?" Ella wondered.

"How can we leave Brookeston? And our tree house? And our friends?" Ethan said.

Ella hugged her knees to her chest. "Hannah will probably find a new best friend while I'm gone."

"Yeah. Theo will probably find someone else to go to the comic-book store with," Ethan mumbled.

The twins grew quiet again. They had a million questions and worries swirling around in their heads—but no answers.

Ethan gazed up at a map of Brookeston on the tree house wall. Their school was just down the street from their house. Also nearby were some of their favorite spots: the playground, the duck pond, and the big fountain in the town square where they made wishes.

Next to the map of their town, the map of the world seemed so much bigger. And so much scarier . . .

"Hello?"

Someone was coming

up the rope ladder. A moment later, Mr. Briar's head appeared in the doorway.

"What's the password?!" the twins shouted at the same time.

"Um . . . uh . . . spaghetti and meat-balls?" Mr. Briar guessed.

"Wrong!" Ethan replied.

"I actually just came out here to get you guys. It's early bedtime tonight. Your mom wants us to spend the day tomorrow packing," Mr. Briar explained.

Ella looked at her brother. "Maybe when we wake up tomorrow, we'll realize this was just a dream," she said hopefully.

Ethan tried to smile. "Yeah, maybe."

CHAPTER 3

A Visitor!

Exactly one week later, Ella woke up with a start. It hadn't been a dream—the Briars were moving the next day. Ella barely recognized her bedroom. There were boxes everywhere. Boxes of books. Boxes of clothes. Boxes of toys and other things, like her seashell and shark teeth collections.

The Briars had spent much of the

past week sorting their belongings into two categories: stuff they would take with them on their trip around the world and stuff they would put away in the attic.

While they were gone, another family was going to rent the house. Ella tried to picture a strange kid taking over her room. What if he or she was a baby who covered Ella's desk with stickers? That desk was where Ella sat and wrote all her mystery stories—including her latest one, "The Case of the Missing Diamond."

Ella sighed and got out of bed.

The doorbell rang downstairs. A moment later Mrs. Briar yelled, *"Ella! Ethan!* There's someone here to see you!"

Ella went out into the hallway. She saw that Ethan's door was still closed. She used their secret knock: three quick knocks, a pause, and then three more

quick knocks. It was code for "hi."

"Ethan? Are you awake?" she called out.

"No," came the reply from inside.

Ella opened the door and went in. Ethan was in bed, buried under his soccer-ball sheets. His room was a maze of boxes.

"Mom says we have a visitor," Ella said.

"I'm sleeping," came Ethan's voice from under the sheets.

Ella glanced around. "You still have a lot of packing to do."

Ethan poked his head out. His wavy brown hair was sticking up. "That's part of my brilliant plan. I'm not going to finish packing. That way, we'll miss our plane tomorrow."

Ella considered this. "I don't think that'll work. Mom is really organized. She'll make you finish packing."

Ethan groaned.

"Come on, Ethan," Ella said.

Downstairs, their surprise guest was waiting for them in the living room.

"Grandpa Harry!" Ethan and Ella shouted. They rushed into his arms and gave him a big hug. Grandpa Harry lived in Fall Creek, which was the next town over. The twins saw him at least once a week.

"God morgon!" Grandpa Harry said merrily. He always greeted them in a different foreign language.

"Is that German?" Ethan guessed.

"Close. It's Swedish. Did I ever tell you kids about the time your grandmother and I stayed in a hotel in Sweden that was made entirely of ice?"

"Didn't it melt in the summer?" Ella asked.

"Didn't you and Grandma freeze?" Ethan piped up at the same time.

Grandpa Harry laughed. "They rebuilt the hotel every winter. And no, we didn't freeze. But enough about me. I hear you kids are starting your big adventure tomorrow!"

The twins stopped smiling.

Grandpa Harry knelt down in front of them. "What's the matter, my dears?" he asked gently.

"We . . . we don't want to go," Ella confessed.

"I understand," Grandpa Harry said. "It's hard to leave everything you know behind. But guess what?"

"What?" Ella and Ethan asked.

"Life is all about adventures," Grandpa Harry replied. "And there is a whole world out there for you to discover. A world full of ice hotels, castles, ancient ruins . . . I could go on and on. Brookeston will always be

here, waiting for you. Your house will be here. *I'll* be here."

The twins nodded slowly.

"Oh, I almost forgot!" Grandpa Harry reached into his jacket and pulled out two packages. "I have some *bon voyage* presents for you."

Ella knew that *bon voyage* meant "have a good trip!" in French. Her mom used to say that to Grandpa Harry and Grandma Lucy whenever they left for a new destination.

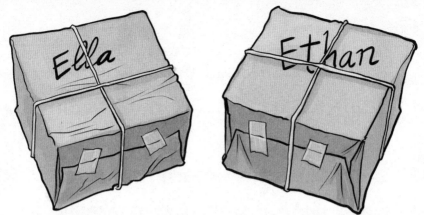

Ethan opened his present right away. Inside was a box containing an old-fashioned-looking gold coin. It had a picture of a globe on one side and a hawk on the other.

"Cool!" he said, grinning. "Thanks, Grandpa! What does the coin mean—"

But Ethan was interrupted by a gasp from Ella.

"Thank you, Grandpa Harry!" Ella

exclaimed. She had opened her present. It was a journal with a beautiful purple cover.

"I know how much you love to write, Ella," Grandpa Harry replied. "I thought you could use this to take notes on your travels. It might come in handy for solving mysteries, too."

"Solving mysteries?" Ella asked.

"What do you mean?" Ethan piped up curiously.

Grandpa Harry winked at the kids. "I've learned that when you start a big adventure, you never know when a mystery might land in your path."

CHAPTER 4

The Missing Coin on Moving Day

"We have to be at the airport at four p.m.," Mrs. Briar said over Sunday brunch the next day. "Our taxi will be here at three to pick us up."

Ethan glanced at his watch. It was almost noon.

They were having a farewell brunch with Grandpa Harry. Mr. Briar had made pancakes. Grandpa Harry had brought strawberries from a nearby farmers' market.

"Let's figure out our schedules for the next few hours," Mrs. Briar went on. "I have to pick up some last-minute things at the mall. Andy, can you finish up the cleaning? And, Dad, can you supervise the kids? I made a to-do list for them."

Uh-oh, Ethan thought. *One of Mom's famous to-do lists.*

"I'd be glad to help them," Grandpa Harry said.

Mrs. Briar handed the to-do list to Ethan and Ella. It was about a mile long. Ethan felt dizzy just reading the

TO DO

-Pack your backpacks with activities for the plane.

-Check your closets and make sure they're empty.

-Ditto dresser drawers

-Ditto bookshelves

-Ditto under your beds

-Ditto the basement playroom

-Tape up all boxes labeled with your names.

list. How were they going to get all this done?

Mr. Briar began clearing the dishes. Brunch was over. The day was flying by. Ethan wasn't ready to get up and go.

He dug into the pockets of his Brookeston Boomers hoodie. "Oh, no!" he cried out.

"What's the matter?" Ella asked him.

Ethan felt around in his pockets some more. Still empty. "My gold coin! It's gone!"

"It's probably in your room," Ella said.

"No. I know I had it when we went

downtown yesterday. I was wearing this exact same hoodie," Ethan said worriedly.

Grandpa Harry leaned across the table. "Sounds like a mystery to me," he said with a twinkle in his eye.

"A mystery? We don't have *time* for a mystery," Ethan complained.

"Of course you do. Why don't you give me your to-do list, and I'll start tackling it. While I'm doing that, the two of you can look for the gold coin," Grandpa Harry offered.

With that, he took the list from the twins. He pulled his glasses out of

his jacket pocket and headed for the stairs, humming to himself.

Ethan turned to Ella. "*Now* what? I just want my coin back!"

"Okay, let's think. We spent the whole day yesterday running errands with Dad. Maybe you dropped it along the way," Ella suggested.

"*Great.* It could be anywhere!" Ethan wailed.

Ella's brown eyes lit up. "Not *anywhere.*"

She reached for her new journal and a pen. She opened it up to the first page and began to write. "Let's see. Yesterday, we went to the bakery first," she said. "Then the bead store, then

the bookstore, then the comic-book store."

"What are you doing?" Ethan asked.

"You mean, what are *we* doing? *We* are going to retrace our steps from yesterday and find your gold coin!" Ella said excitedly.

CHAPTER 5

And the Search Begins

"First stop: Petunia Bakery," Ella announced.

A tiny bell jingled as she and Ethan opened the door. Inside the shop, the smell of freshly baked cookies made their mouths water.

The bakery and the rest of downtown Brookeston were only a few blocks from the Briars' house. With

Mrs. Briar at the mall and Mr. Briar busy cleaning, it had been easy for the twins to sneak away. Grandpa Harry had wished them luck and gone back to taping up boxes as the twins left.

Mrs. Valentine, the baker, waved at them from behind the cash register. As always, the glass counter was filled

with cupcakes, pies, and lots of other yummy-looking treats.

"I thought you'd left for your trip," she called out.

"We're leaving at three o'clock," Ella replied.

Then Mrs. Valentine held out two chocolate-chip cookies. "How about a

cookie on the house as a *bon voyage* present?"

The twins were at the counter in about two seconds flat. As Ella bit into the delicious cookie, she opened up her journal. "Mrs. Valentine, when we were here yesterday, Ethan may have dropped a gold coin. Have you seen it?" she asked.

"It has a globe on one side and a hawk on the other," Ethan told the baker.

"No, I haven't seen anything like that. Let me check in the lost-and-found box." Mrs. Valentine dipped her head behind the counter and rummaged around.

While Mrs. Valentine was busy, Ella and Ethan searched the rest of the shop. They peered under tables and chairs. They scanned tall shelves packed with jams, jellies, and teas. They looked through the window display.

By the time they were done, Ethan had found a couple of pennies and Ella had found a rhinestone hairpin—but no gold coin.

They brought the hairpin up to Mrs. Valentine.

"Goodness, I've been looking for that everywhere!" she exclaimed. "Sometimes you think you've lost something forever. But it turns out, it's right under your nose! Thank you so much, children!"

"You're welcome!" Ella said.

"I'm afraid your coin isn't in my lost-and-found box," Mrs. Valentine apologized. "But I will e-mail your parents if I come across it."

Ella and Ethan thanked the baker and said good-bye. Before they left, Ella opened up her journal and jotted down some notes:

We didn't find the gold coin at Petunia Bakery.

We did find Mrs. Valentine's hairpin, though.

She said: "Sometimes you think you've lost something forever. But it turns out, it's right under your nose."

CHAPTER 6

Best Friends and a Soccer Ball

Ethan and Ella headed over to Bead Mania next. It was Ella's favorite store in Brookeston. Ethan had no idea why. Who cared about making bracelets and stuff, anyway?

"Um, maybe you should go inside alone," Ethan suggested. "I'll search the perimeter. You know, that means the outside part," he added quickly.

"I know what 'perimeter' means," Ella snapped. "Fine, then. I'll just go inside and investigate by myself. 'Investigate' means look around."

"I *know* that," Ethan said, rolling his eyes.

Ella headed into the store. Ethan decided to start with the flower garden in front. He got down on his knees and squinted at the dirt beneath the plants. He wished he had a metal detector. He saw an ant, a worm, and a ladybug—but no coin.

"Hey! Ethan!"

Ethan glanced up. His best friend, Theo, stood on the sidewalk, holding a soccer ball.

The two boys had said good-bye to each other on Friday after their game against the Fall Creek Falcons. Still, it was nice to run into Theo one last time.

"Hi!" Ethan rose to his feet. "Is there a game today?"

"Nah. I went to the park to kick the ball around. Nobody was there, though." Theo looked away.

Ethan felt bad. He and Theo often went to that park together to play soccer on the weekends.

"So what are you doing?" Theo pointed to the flower garden.

"I'm looking for my gold coin. My grandpa gave it to me as a going-away present. But I dropped it some-where yesterday," Ethan explained.

"Wow! Is there anything I can do to help? What does it look like?" Theo asked.

"Well . . . it's about the size of a quarter. It has a globe on one side and a hawk on the other," Ethan replied.

Theo thought for a moment. "I have a gold coin in my coin collection. It's an old train token. I actually thought it was a quarter. It doesn't have a

globe or a hawk on it, though."

Just then, Ella came out of Bead Mania.

"Sorry it took so long. I didn't find your coin." She turned to Theo. "Oh, hi! Are you here to buy some beads?"

"No way," Theo replied. "I'm on my way home. I have to study for that math test tomorrow."

"We'd better go, too," Ella said to Ethan. "We still have two more stores on our list."

"Yeah," Ethan agreed. "Bye again," he said sadly.

"Bye, Eth," Theo replied.

Just then, Theo tossed his soccer ball at Ethan. Ethan returned it with a perfect header. Theo jumped up in the air and caught it neatly.

The two boys laughed and waved good-bye.

"I hope you find your coin!" Theo called out.

Ethan hoped so, too. *Soon.*

CHAPTER 7
A Little Bit of Luck?

Ella and Ethan's next stop was the Wise Owl bookstore.

"I guess you two didn't buy enough books when you were here with your dad yesterday," Mr. DeMarco joked when the twins walked in.

On Saturday, Ella, Ethan, and their dad had picked up some books for the trip. Ella had selected *The Secret Garden*.

Ethan had chosen *The Borrowers*.

"Actually, we are here to solve a mystery," Ella told Mr. DeMarco.

Mr. DeMarco pushed his glasses up on his nose. "A mystery? You mean like something from a Nancy Drew or Hardy Boys story?"

"Exactly!" Ella said. "Ethan's gold

coin disappeared yesterday, so we're retracing our steps."

"I may have dropped it here," Ethan added.

"A gold coin? Hmm . . . I don't think I've seen one of those lately," Mr. DeMarco said. "But let me look in my cash register. Maybe it got mixed in with the other coins somehow."

"Is it okay if we look around for it?" Ethan asked.

"Of course! Take all the time you need," Mr. DeMarco replied.

Ella and Ethan agreed to split up to search for the coin. Ella would take the kids' books room, and Ethan would take the main room.

Once she was in the kids' room, Ella searched everywhere. But there was no sign of Ethan's coin.

A girl with red braids wandered into the room. Her face was buried in a book.

"Hannah?" Ella called out.

The girl glanced up. It *was* Hannah!

"Ella!" Hannah exclaimed.

The two girls rushed up to each other and hugged.

"What are you doing here?" cried Hannah. "I thought you were gone!"

"We're leaving this afternoon," Ella told her.

Hannah sighed. "I'm going to miss you so much! What's going to happen to our book club? And our poetry club?" She and Ella were always coming up with fun clubs for just the two of them.

"Well, we can e-mail our poems to each other. And we can e-mail about the books we read, too," Ella said.

Hannah nodded eagerly. "Yes! And you have to tell me about all the places you visit. And send lots of photos, too. I am *so* jealous!"

"You are?" Ella asked, surprised.

Hannah nodded. "You're taking a trip around the world. You're the

luckiest person I know!" she exclaimed.

The girls exchanged one last hug before Hannah left to meet up with her mom. Ella took a minute to sit down on a beanbag chair and write in her journal.

I ran into Hannah at the bookstore. I'll miss her a lot.
     She says I'm really lucky to be going on a trip around the world.
     I'm starting to wonder if maybe I am . . .

Just then, Ethan rushed into the kids' room.

"Hey, Ella! Guess what?" he said excitedly.

CHAPTER 8

A Bright Idea

"Did you find your coin?" Ella asked her brother.

Ethan shook his head. "No, but I just thought of something! Theo told me he added a train token to his coin collection by accident because he thought it was a quarter."

"So?" Ella responded.

"So what if someone found my coin

and didn't look at it carefully? Maybe they thought it was a quarter, too," Ethan said.

"That's a good idea," Ella replied.

The twins said good-bye again to Mr. DeMarco and left the store. They made a quick stop at Galaxy Comics next door, just to make sure the gold coin wasn't there. It wasn't—although the storeowner, Mr. Max, gave Ethan a new comic book as a *bon voyage* present.

Ethan glanced at his watch as they left the comic-book store. The twins had less than half an hour to find the coin and get home.

They turned the corner and found themselves in the town square. It was a sunny spring day, and everyone seemed to be out. On one side of the big fountain, a man played jazz music on his saxophone. People stopped by to listen. They tossed coins into his

open saxophone case.

Coins . . .

"Ella!" Ethan said in a low voice. "What if someone found my coin and gave it to the saxophone player?"

Ella's eyes widened. "Let's go check it out!"

The twins rushed over to the musician. They squeezed through the crowd to get closer to the case.

Ethan bent down. No gold coin.

The musician looked over at Ethan suspiciously. Did he think Ethan was a thief?

"My coin's not in there. Let's keep looking," Ethan whispered to Ella.

"Hey, Ethan? I've been thinking about something Mrs. Valentine said," Ella remarked as they walked away. She pulled out her journal and opened it to the second page. She pointed to what she had written.

"'Sometimes you think you've lost something forever. But it turns out, it's right under your nose,'" Ethan read.

He thought about this. "What does 'under your nose' mean?"

"It means that something you've lost might be closer than you think," Ella told him. "Maybe your coin is right under our noses, and we just don't know it."

"Ethan! Ella!"

Their neighbor Mrs. Sanchez waved to them from a bench. Her dog, Sugarplum, bounded up to the twins, wagging her tail. Ethan and Ella had known Sugarplum since she was a puppy.

"Hi, Mrs. Sanchez! Hi, Sugarplum!" Ethan said as the twins joined Mrs. Sanchez on the bench.

"Are you here to make a wish before you leave for your trip?" Mrs. Sanchez asked.

"Huh?" Ethan asked, puzzled.

"At the fountain," Mrs. Sanchez said with a chuckle. "The two of you have been throwing pennies and making wishes since you were old enough to walk. Why, I remember—"

"Ella, that's it!" Ethan practically shouted. "It's right under our noses!"

Ella glanced around wildly. "It is? Where?"

"What are you two talking about?" Mrs. Sanchez asked, confused.

"We'll explain later. Come on, Ella!"

Ethan jumped to his feet and began weaving through the crowd.

Ella followed. "Where are we going now?" she asked her brother.

"To the fountain!" Ethan cried.

When they reached the fountain, Ethan leaned over and peered inside. He circled it once, twice, three times.

There were hundreds of coins lying on the bottom. The water glittered like a quilt of silver and copper.

Ethan swished his hand through the cool water. He saw pennies, nickels, dimes, and quarters—but no gold coins.

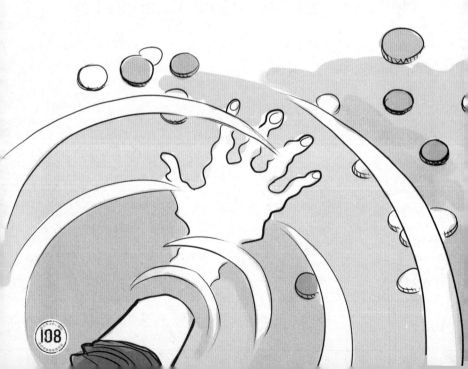

"I don't think we're allowed to do that," Ella said nervously.

"Just trust me," Ethan replied.

A church bell tolled in the distance. Ethan glanced at his watch again. It was 2:45. They had to get home or they'd miss their flight!

A cloud passed over the sun. Suddenly a shimmer of gold caught Ethan's eye.

"A gold coin!" Ethan cried out.

He reached into the fountain. He pulled out the coin and studied it closely.

On one side was a globe . . . and on the other was a hawk. It was his coin! He grinned and showed it to Ella.

The twins high-fived each other. Mystery solved!

CHAPTER 9
The Last Good-bye

Ella and Ethan got home just as their mom's car pulled into the driveway.

Mrs. Briar emerged with an armful of shopping bags. "I'm sorry that took so long," she apologized.

The twins exchanged a glance. Mrs. Briar obviously had no idea that they'd been gone for the past few hours.

"Oh, that's okay, Mom," Ella said, trying to catch her breath.

"Yeah, Mom. No problem," Ethan added.

Mrs. Briar gave them a suspicious look. "Did you get everything done on your list? Please tell me you did."

"Um . . . ," Ethan and Ella began.

"*Sure* they did!"

Grandpa Harry stepped through the front door holding a cardboard box. "Come have some lemonade before you leave!" he called out cheerfully.

Mr. Briar came outside, too. His face and hands were smudged with dirt.

"Hi, Jo. Hey, kids! Sorry I couldn't help with your list. The basement cleanup took longer than I thought."

"Andy, you're a mess! Why, we're going to have to do a cleanup on *you*," Mrs. Briar joked.

Mr. and Mrs. Briar went inside the

house. Ella and Ethan rushed up to Grandpa Harry with big smiles on their faces.

Ethan opened his fist and showed Grandpa Harry the gold coin.

"I knew you two could do it," Grandpa Harry said with a wink.

* * *

The taxi was early. It sat in the driveway while Ethan, Ella, and their parents scrambled around the house to make sure they had everything.

"You're ready. You've got everything. Now, *go!*" Grandpa Harry ordered the four of them not much later. "I'll do a last sweep after you're gone."

"All right." Mrs. Briar gave him a hug. "I'll e-mail you as soon as we get there."

"*Bon voyage*, JoJo," said Grandpa Harry.

Mrs. Briar brushed back a tear. "Thanks, Dad. Love you!"

Ethan and Ella stood frozen in their spots. Grandpa Harry leaned down and patted them on their heads.

"I don't want to say good-bye," Ella said, choking back a sob.

"I don't want to say good-bye, either." Ethan sniffled.

"Then let's say *arrivederci* instead," Grandpa Harry suggested.

"What does that mean?" the twins asked.

"It's Italian for 'see you again,'" their grandfather explained.

A few minutes later, the family piled into the taxi. As it pulled out of the driveway, Ella and Ethan turned around in their seats.

Grandpa Harry stood on the lawn,

waving. The twins waved back.

"*Arrivederci,*" they whispered.

They kept waving until they couldn't see Grandpa Harry anymore.

Ella clutched her journal.

Ethan held his gold coin tightly.

After all that, both Ella and Ethan really were excited about the big new adventure that was about to unfold. They had sights to see . . . people to meet . . . and, maybe, just maybe, more mysteries to solve.

GREETINGS FROM SOMEWHERE

The Mystery of the Mosaic

#2

TABLE OF CONTENTS

CHAPTER 1
The Floating City

Ella Briar and her twin brother, Ethan, had never been to Venice, Italy, before. They'd never been to a floating city, either!

Venice was made up of a bunch of tiny islands connected by canals and bridges. The canals were like streets, except filled with water. So some people were using boats to get around, and others were walking over the bridges from one little street to another!

The Briar family had traveled by water taxi from the airport. The sleek motorboat pulled up to a cream-colored building with lots of balconies.

"Here's our hotel!" the twins' mother, Josephine Briar, said brightly.

PENSIONE MISTERO

Their dad, Andrew, pushed his glasses up on his nose and pointed to his guidebook. "It says here that the Pensione Mistero is one of the oldest hotels in Venice."

"Is it older than you guys?" Ella asked with a sneaky smile.

Mr. Briar laughed. "I should hope so. It was built more than eight hundred years ago."

The four of them stepped out of the boat with their suitcases. Pink, yellow, and pale green buildings lined both sides of the canal. Pretty flowers and vines filled the window boxes. There

were no cars or bicycles on the cobble-stone streets, only people walking.

For a moment, Ella and Ethan were so awed by their surroundings that they forgot they were supposed to be sad. Or mad. Or sad *and* mad.

Just yesterday, they had said good-bye to everything and everyone they loved: their house in Brookeston, their friends, their school, and most of all, their Grandpa Harry. Their

mom was starting her new job as a travel writer. That meant she had to travel to different foreign cities and write about them for her newspaper column, Journeys with Jo!

It also meant the rest of the family had to travel with her. Ella and Ethan had *not* been happy about that. While Mrs. Briar was out researching and writing, Mr. Briar would be homeschooling the twins.

When the Briars entered the hotel, a woman greeted them from the front desk.

"*Buon giorno!* Hello! I am Sofia," she said cheerfully. She handed the Briars a large gold key and told them their rooms were on the fourth floor.

There was no elevator, so the family climbed up the narrow, twisting staircase. 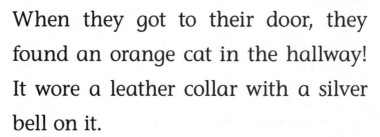 When they got to their door, they found an orange cat in the hallway! It wore a leather collar with a silver bell on it.

"Hi. Who are you?" Ella smiled and bent down to look at it. It purred and rubbed against her leg.

"It probably doesn't understand English," Ethan said. "You should speak Italian."

"I'm sure this kitty doesn't care what language you speak as long as you pet it," Mrs. Briar joked.

"I'm going to call you 'Pumpkin'

because you look like a cute little pumpkin," Ella told the cat.

Pumpkin meowed.

The Briars went inside using the gold key, and Pumpkin followed. The living room had tall ceilings, antique furniture, and a view of the canal.

There were two bedrooms and a small kitchen too.

Ella thought about her room back in Brookeston. She thought about her seashell and shark tooth collections.

She thought about Grandma Lucy's old desk, where she wrote her poems and short stories. She thought about the tree house in the backyard.

Then she tried to push all those thoughts out of her mind. *This* was their new home now—well, at least for the next few weeks it was. She and Ethan would just have to make the most of it.

CHAPTER 2

The Two Hawks

"I think our restaurant is right around the next corner," Mr. Briar said, squinting at a map of Venice.

It was dinnertime, and the Briars were headed to a place called the Marco Polo Ristorante. Grandpa Harry had recommended it to them.

Ethan and Ella followed their dad along a crowded street lined with shops and cafés. Their mom trailed after them in her high-heeled shoes. She was talking to someone on her cell phone about the Doge's Palace.

"Hey, Dad? What is the Doge's Palace?" Ella asked.

"A long time ago, Venice was ruled by someone called a 'doge.' A doge was elected by the people of Venice to lead the city for his entire lifetime. Now the palace is a sight for visitors like us." Mr. Briar was a history professor and knew interesting stuff like that.

A few minutes later, they reached the Marco Polo Ristorante. Inside, the air smelled  yummy, like garlic and tomato sauce. Black-and-white photographs and flickering candles lined the brick walls.

"Why are lots of places in Venice named Marco Polo something?" Ethan wondered out loud. He remembered that the airport was called the Marco Polo Airport. He also remembered seeing a sign for the Hotel Marco Polo. Marco Polo was his absolute favorite

swimming pool game, too!

"Marco Polo was a famous explorer. He was born in Venice," Mr. Briar explained.

A tall man in a tuxedo came up to them. "*Buona sera!* Good evening! Do you have a reservation?"

"We do!" Mrs. Briar said, closing her cell phone. "Briar, table for four. My father, Harry Robinson, used to come to your restaurant a long time ago," she told the man.

"Of course! Signor Robinson is a dear friend," the man said affectionately. "My name is Luigi. Please, come right this way."

Luigi led them to a table overlooking

the canal. Ella thought the water looked beautiful at night. Ethan peered out the window. Outside, there was an old stone bridge with a dock underneath. There was a long black and green boat tied to the dock. Ethan admired it through the glass. He noticed a small gold ornament on the front of it, but from his angle, he couldn't quite make out what it was.

Luigi saw Ethan looking at the boat. "That boat is called a gondola. It belongs to my son, Antonio," he explained. "It has been in our family for many generations. *Antonio!*"

A young man with curly dark hair rushed over to their table with menus.

"Antonio, this is the family of my friend Harry Robinson—the one from America," Luigi told his son.

Antonio's eyes widened. "Oh! This is a very great honor!"

Ella leaned toward Ethan. "They must *really* like Grandpa Harry," she whispered.

Ethan nodded. Grandpa Harry was a famous archaeologist. Archaeologists studied people

from the ancient past by looking at the things they left behind, such as artwork and old buildings. Like Marco Polo, Grandpa Harry once traveled around the world exploring for his work.

Grandpa Harry must have met Luigi

and Antonio on one of his trips, Ethan thought.

Antonio started to hand the Briars their menus. But his father grabbed them and clutched them to his chest. "No menus! I will prepare a special meal just for you," Luigi announced to the Briars. "A little mozzarella, maybe some pasta à la carbonara . . ." He turned and rushed off to the kitchen.

"Mr. Antonio? What's that gold thing on the front of your boat?" Ethan asked curiously.

"Every gondola has an ornament.

Mine is a . . . well, I believe the word is 'hawk' in English," Antonio replied.

"Really?" Ethan reached into his pocket and pulled out his prized gold coin from Grandpa Harry. It had a globe on one side . . . and a hawk on the other!

Huh, Ethan thought. But before he could say anything, Antonio spoke.

"Perhaps I could take you all for a ride in my gondola during your stay," he suggested. "It is hundreds of years old and used to belong to one of the doges of Venice."

"Yes, please!" Ethan and Ella said eagerly.

Maybe Venice wouldn't be such a bad place to spend a little time, after all!

CHAPTER 3
A Mysterious E-mail

The next day Ella and Ethan slept way past their usual wake-up time.

"It's late!" Ethan announced from his bed across the room. "We missed breakfast!"

Ella opened her eyes and sat up in her bed. Bright sunlight streamed through the large window. A warm breeze rustled the lace curtains. Next

to her, Pumpkin
stirred on the
velvety green
quilt, purring.
The Briars
had learned
from Sofia
that Pumpkin
used to be
a stray but
lived at the hotel now.

Someone knocked on the door.
Mr. Briar stuck his head inside. He
wore jeans and a T-shirt with the red,
white, and green flag of Italy on it.

"Good morning! I wanted to let you guys sleep in a bit," he said cheerfully.

"Where's Mom?" Ethan asked.

"She's at the library doing research for her column. I thought the three of us could go out for some *gelato*." Mr. Briar added, "That's the Italians' ice cream!"

Ella and Ethan laughed. Their dad *loved* trying foreign foods.

"Can I check some e-mail first?" Ella

asked. She really missed her friends
back home. Maybe one of them had
sent her a message.

"Yeah, me too!" Ethan said. The
twins shared an e-mail address.

"Of course! My computer is on the
desk," Mr. Briar replied.

Ella and Ethan hurried to the living
room. Their dad's laptop sat on a fancy
wooden desk with cool designs carved
into it. They raced to the leather chair
and scrunched onto it together.

Ethan opened their e-mail account.

There were three messages waiting for them.

The first was from Ethan's best friend, Theo, telling him about the Brookeston Boomers' soccer game against the Trumansburg Titans. The second was a message from Ella's best friend, Hannah, with a new poem she had written for their poetry club.

The third and final message was from Grandpa Harry. The subject line of his e-mail was: TWO CLUES.

"What does that mean? Two clues to what?" Ethan asked.

"I don't know," Ella replied. "Let's find out!"

Ethan clicked to open the e-mail from Grandpa Harry.

Hello, my dears. *Benvenuti a Venezia!* (That means "Welcome to Venice!")

Venice is one of my favorite cities in the world. Your Grandma Lucy and I visited it many times when she was alive.

She and I loved the churches and the museums there. We also loved the many bridges over the canals, like the Rialto Bridge and the Bridge of Sighs. But perhaps our absolute favorite thing in Venice was a five-hundred-year-old mosaic. (A mosaic is a type of artwork made up of lots of little pieces of glass in different colors.)

You should try to find this very special mosaic. However, it will not be easy!

I can offer you two clues to get you started:

1) Calle Farnese

2) Look up!

I know from your last mystery that you are very good at finding things. Good luck!

Lots of love,

Grandpa Harry

PS Say hello to my old friend Luigi and his son, Antonio, for me! I hope Antonio will show you his beautiful gondola, which used to belong to a doge of Venice.

Ethan glanced up from the screen. "We have to find the mosaic!" he told Ella excitedly.

"I know. But how? And who's this Calle Farnese person?" Ella said, puzzled.

"I'm not sure. Why don't you write down those clues in the notebook Grandpa Harry gave you?" Ethan suggested.

The day before their trip, Grandpa Harry had given both of the twins going-away presents.

Ethan's was the gold coin with the hawk on it. Ella's was a purple notebook. Grandpa Harry had told her that it might 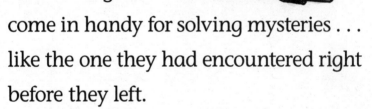 come in handy for solving mysteries . . . like the one they had encountered right before they left.

Ethan's coin had disappeared just hours before the Briars had to get to the airport. The twins had used Ella's notebook to keep track of clues and other information. At the last minute, they'd found the coin in quite an unexpected place.

Now it seemed they had a *new* mystery to solve!

CHAPTER 4

A Gondola Thief?

"Mmm. This is the best ice cream—I mean *gelato*—I've ever had!" Ethan said, licking his spoon.

Ella finished up the last of her *pesca* gelato. *Pesca* was Italian for "peach." "Me too!"

The twins were strolling through the crowded Piazza San Marco with their father. The piazza was an enormous square with beautiful old buildings along the sides of it. One of the buildings was the Doge's Palace, which Mrs. Briar planned to write about.

"See that church? That's the Basilica San Marco, or St. Mark's Cathedral," Mr. Briar said, pointing. "That tall tower over there is called the Campanile di San Marco. *Campanile* means 'clock tower.' Or is it 'bell tower'? Wait. Let me check."

While Mr. Briar flipped through his guidebook, Ella scanned the crowded square. Nearby, an old man tossed bread crumbs to pigeons. With his

kind face and bushy gray hair, he reminded Ella of Grandpa Harry.

Ella pulled her purple notebook out of her pocket. She glanced at the page on which she'd written Grandpa Harry's clues about Calle Farnese and looking up. What did they mean?

"Bell tower!" Mr. Briar announced

suddenly. "The clock tower is that building, to the north. And speaking of clocks, it's almost two thirty. Let's get back to our hotel so we can dig into the wonderful world of multiplication."

Ella and Ethan groaned. With homeschooling to do, when would

they find time to solve their new mystery?

Mr. Briar led the way across the piazza and onto a side street. They went over a short stone bridge.

As their dad stopped to research the name of the bridge, Ella and Ethan peered over the side. Just up the canal, a red-haired man stood on a dock next to a black and green gondola. He peered around as if to see if anyone was watching him.

Then the man jumped into the gondola and untied it from the dock. He paddled quickly away.

"What just happened?" Ethan asked Ella, puzzled.

"I don't know. Do you think he stole that gondola?" Ella said worriedly.

Ethan frowned. "It sure looked suspicious to me. . . ."

CHAPTER 5

Calle Farnese

When they got back to their hotel room, Mr. Briar had an important message waiting for him. He made a quick call on his cell phone, then turned to Ethan and Ella.

"Bad news," he announced. "That was the passport office. I have to go over there to straighten out a problem with our passports. I'm afraid the

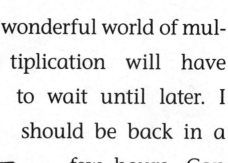

wonderful world of multiplication will have to wait until later. I should be back in a few hours. Can you two find something to keep you busy while I'm gone?"

"Sure, Dad," Ella said.

"Yeah, no problem," Ethan added, trying not to smile.

Mr. Briar threw some things into a bag and left. As soon as he was gone, Ethan went over to the desk and started looking through the messy pile of books and papers.

"What are you looking for?" Ella asked him.

"A map of Venice I saw earlier," Ethan replied.

Ella put her hands on her hips. "But why?"

"Because this is our chance to sneak out and look for Grandpa Harry's mosaic!" Ethan declared. "We should go back to that bridge, too. Where

the gondola was."

Ella frowned. "Are you sure it's okay for us to go out without telling Mom and Dad anything?"

"Just trust me," Ethan assured her.

"Okay, but if we get in trouble, I'm telling them it was *your* idea," Ella insisted. While Ethan searched for the map, Ella glanced around the room. "Where's Pumpkin?"

"She's probably downstairs," Ethan

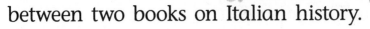

replied without looking up.

A few minutes later, Ethan found the map. It was sandwiched between two books on Italian history. He spread it out on the desk and found the Pensione Mistero on it. He marked it with a big X so they would be able to trace their way back.

Then he noticed something else. "Ella, look! Check this out!"

Ella leaned over the

map. Ethan pointed to a bunch of different streets.

They were all called Calle something. Calle de Mezo, Calle Vinanti, Calle Farnese . . .

Calle Farnese was one of the clues in Grandpa Harry's e-mail!

"Calle Farnese isn't a person. It's a street!" Ella exclaimed.

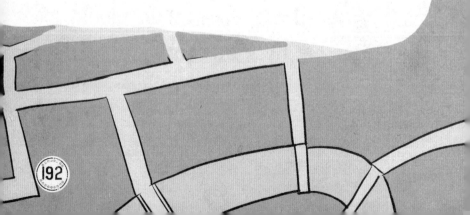

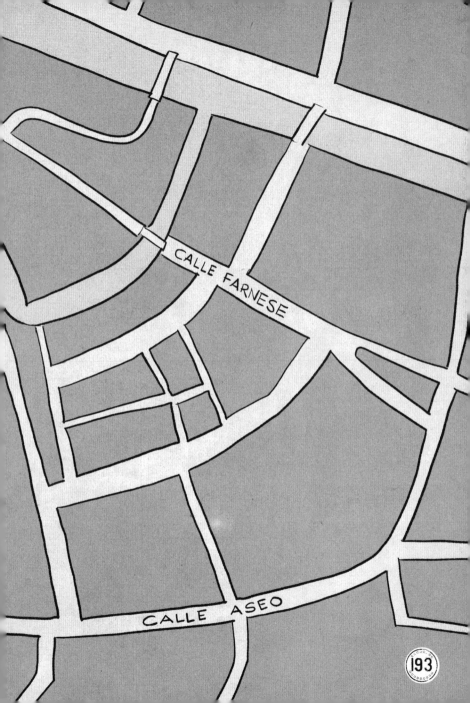

CALLE FARNESE

CALLE ASEO

CHAPTER 6
Pumpkin in Trouble

"I think it's this way," Ella said, pointing to the right.

She and Ethan followed the sidewalk along the canal. Their plan was to retrace their steps back to the stone bridge, then go to Calle Farnese after that. According to the map, Calle Farnese was on the other side of Piazza San Marco. The route there looked complicated, with lots of tiny, winding streets.

They soon reached the stone bridge. Two dark-haired men were standing at the dock where the black and green gondola had been. They seemed to be arguing.

One of the men looked familiar. "That's Antonio!" Ethan said, surprised.

The building just beyond the dock suddenly looked familiar, too. "That's the Marco Polo Ristorante!" Ella added. She hadn't recognized the restaurant before.

Then something else clicked into place as the twins turned toward each other, wide-eyed.

The missing black and green boat must be Antonio's gondola!

Ella and Ethan rushed across the bridge and made their way over to the dock. The two men stopped arguing. "Harry Robinson's grandchildren, what are you doing here?" Antonio asked them.

"We saw someone take your boat, Mr. Antonio," Ella blurted out.

"You see? I *told* you I did not steal it," the other man said angrily to Antonio.

"I should not have jumped to conclusions, Paolo. I am very sorry," Antonio told the other man. "When did this happen? And what did the person look like?" he asked Ella and Ethan.

"He had red hair. And we saw him take it about half an hour ago," Ethan replied.

"We must find this red-haired thief! Will you help me?" Antonio pleaded.

"We can go in my gondola," Paolo offered.

"Yes! We will take you on your very first gondola ride!" Antonio told the twins.

"Sure!" Ethan said excitedly. Ella nodded.

The four of them got into Paolo's gondola, which was tied to a nearby dock. "Which way did this man go?" Paolo asked the twins.

"Straight ahead," Ella said.

Paolo picked up an oar and began paddling. The long boat glided smoothly under the bridge and down the canal. They passed a bookstore and a bustling café. It was like riding in a canoe, but instead of being on a lake, they were in the middle of a busy city!

Ella pulled her purple notebook out of her bag and opened it to a fresh page. She got a pen out of her pocket and began writing.

A red-haired man stole Mr. Antonio's gondola.
Who is he? And why did he steal it?

Just then, Ella heard a familiar "meow." She glanced up and saw a flash of orange on the sidewalk above the canal.

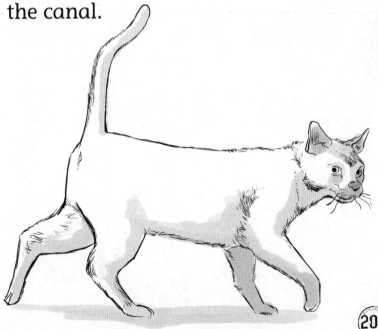

It was Pumpkin!

The little cat ran to the edge of the canal and perched over the water. She howled loudly at Ella and the others in the gondola. Suddenly, Ella saw a dog running toward Pumpkin.

"Mr. Paolo! Stop! Pumpkin is in trouble!" Ella cried out.

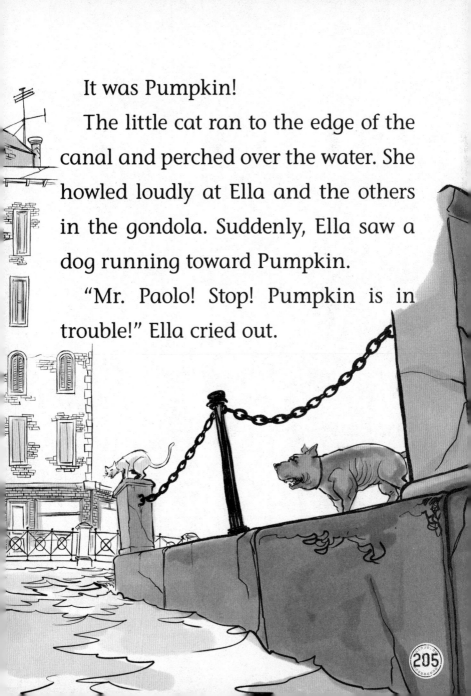

CHAPTER 7

Which Way?

"Pumpkin? I don't see a pumpkin," Paolo said, confused.

"That cat over there!" Ethan told him. "She lives at our hotel."

"Oh!" Paolo steered his gondola over to the sidewalk. Pumpkin jumped right in.

Ella swooped the cat up in her arms.

"I am glad we rescued little *Zucca*—I

mean, Pumpkin. But we must keep going. Otherwise we will lose our thief," Antonio said anxiously.

Paolo continued paddling down the canal. A few minutes later, they reached a fork. The canal branched off to the left and right.

Paolo turned to Antonio. "Which way do we go?"

Antonio frowned. "I am not sure. Perhaps we have lost our thief after all."

"Do you have *any* idea who that

red-haired guy might be?" Ethan asked.

Antonio shook his head.

"Who would want to steal your boat?" Ella piped up. "Do you have any enemies?"

"*Enemies?* Everyone loves Antonio!" Antonio replied.

"Maybe he stole your gondola because it belonged to that famous ruler—a *doge*," Ethan suggested.

Antonio's face lit up. He gasped. "I just remembered something! There was a man who came by to see me at the restaurant last week. He asked where I had gotten my gondola. He said that his grandfather used to own a gondola just like it, but that it was

stolen from him many years ago."
Then Antonio added, "I think the man
had red hair."

"We should go talk to him!" Ella said eagerly. "Do you know his name?"

"No. But he mentioned that his wife owns a glass shop on Calle Rosanna," Antonio said.

"To Calle Rosanna now!" Paolo exclaimed, picking up his oar.

* * *

Ten minutes later, Ethan, Ella, Antonio, and Paolo reached Calle Rosanna. Laundry flapped on a clothesline that stretched from one window to another above the water. Children kicked a soccer ball on the street.

"My gondola! There it is!" Antonio shouted.

Antonio's black and green boat
was docked in front of a tiny shop
with a sign that said: CRISTALLERIA.
Colorful figurines gleamed in the
shop's window. Inside, a woman
shaped a swan out of a hot,

glowing piece of molten glass. Paolo paddled over to the dock. Antonio started to climb out of Paolo's boat and into his own.

Just then, someone ran out of the shop. It was the red-haired man. And he looked angry!

CHAPTER 8
One More Mystery

The red-haired man began shouting in Italian. Antonio shouted back, also in Italian.

"What's happening, Mr. Paolo?" Ella asked. She held Pumpkin tightly in her arms.

"Antonio told the man—I believe his name is Carlo—to give back the gondola. Carlo said no because

the gondola rightly belongs to his grandfather," Paolo translated.

Antonio switched to English just then. "These children saw you steal my gondola!" he told Carlo, pointing to Ethan and Ella.

"You mean my *grandfather's* gondola," Carlo said angrily. "I don't know how your family came to possess it. But after I spoke to you last week, I came straight home and matched it against photographs of my grandfather's boat. They were the same. So I went to the police, but they said I had no real proof! That's why I had to take the gondola back on my own."

"How do you know the two boats are the same?" Ella asked Carlo.

Carlo was startled. "Why, because the details are identical. The black and green colors, the eagle ornament . . ."

"Wait! The ornament on this gondola is a hawk, not an eagle!" Ethan told him.

"What?" Carlo walked around to the front of the boat. He stared closely

at the ornament. Then his shoulders slumped. "You are right. It *is* a hawk ornament. I am very sorry for the confusion," he said to Antonio.

Antonio nodded. "I accept your apology," he said. "You thought you were helping your grandfather."

The two men shook hands. Then Carlo returned to the glass shop, and Antonio got into his gondola.

"*Grazie.* Thank you," Antonio said to Ethan and Ella. "If it hadn't been for you, I would never have found my boat! Now, please . . . let me take you two back to your hotel."

The twins stepped carefully into Antonio's gondola, carrying Pumpkin with them. Paolo waved and paddled off. Antonio began paddling too.

"Mr. Antonio? Can we make a quick stop first?" Ethan asked.

"*Sì!* Yes! Anything for my great

detectives!" Antonio exclaimed.

Ethan pulled the map of Venice out of his pocket. He smoothed it out on his lap and pointed to Calle Farnese. "Can you take us there? We have one more mystery to solve!" he said eagerly.

CHAPTER 9

The Mosaic

"Here we are. Calle Farnese!" Antonio announced a little while later. "I will wait for you with Pumpkin while you solve your mystery. Please be careful. It is easy to get lost in Venice."

"Thank you!" Ella said.

Antonio tied the gondola to a dock. Ella and Ethan stepped out of the gondola. On the side of an old brick building, they saw a black-and-white sign that said CALLE FARNESE. They rushed toward the sign. They were finally going to see the mosaic!

They turned onto Calle Farnese. Apartment buildings lined either side of the street, which was barely wide enough for both of them! Overhead, the twins could make out a thin sliver of blue sky.

Ethan and Ella wandered down the street, searching for the mosaic. They didn't really know where it would be. They looked at doors, through windows, and on walls. They searched all over the ground.

"How are we ever going to find it? We don't even know what it looks like," Ethan complained.

"Grandpa said it was made up of little pieces of colored glass," Ella reminded him.

They continued down Calle Farnese, but the mosaic was nowhere in sight. After a while, they decided it was time to turn around. They had to get back to the hotel before their parents returned and realized they were missing.

"I guess we'll never

find it," Ethan said with a sigh.

"Wait! What about Grandpa's other clue?" Ella reached for her purple notebook and flipped through the pages. "Here. 'Look up.'"

The twins glanced up. But there was only sky, no mosaic.

"Look! Over there!" Ethan cried out suddenly.

Just ahead of them was a short alleyway that turned off to the left. Ella and Ethan ran over to it and tilted their heads to look up.

There it was, high on a wall!

Crafted from tiny bits of colored glass, the mosaic showed a scene of ancient Venice. A glittering glass palace stood on the banks of a glittering glass harbor. A king and queen rode on a gondola through the turquoise

glass water. An amber bird soared through the brilliant blue sky.

It was the most amazing thing they had ever seen.

CHAPTER 10

Venezia, Ti Amo

As soon as Ethan and Ella got back to their hotel with Pumpkin, they sat down at the desk to write Grandpa Harry an e-mail. Luckily, their parents were both still out. Ethan began to type.

Dear Grandpa Harry,

Guess what? We found your mosaic! My favorite part was the king. Ella says her favorite part was the sparkly blue water.

We also solved another mystery. We helped Mr. Antonio find his gondola.

Did you know that his boat has a hawk on it? Like the coin you gave me. Hawks are messengers of the sky. They're symbols of nobility, too. Nobility means you come from a rich and powerful family. We looked it up!

We decided that we love solving mysteries. And we love Venice, too! Guess how you say that in Italian? *Venezia, ti amo.*

Love,

Ethan (and Ella)

Just as Ethan hit SEND, the front door opened. Mr. and Mrs. Briar walked in. "Look who I ran into on my way

home from the passport office!"
Mr. Briar said merrily.

"I was walking back and got *so* lost." Mrs. Briar smoothed her blond hair that was tangled from the wind.

"It is very easy to get lost in Venice," Ethan said, imitating Antonio's voice.

Ella giggled.

Their parents exchanged a puzzled glance.

"So what did you kids do while we were gone?" Mrs. Briar asked.

"I hope you weren't too bored," Mr. Briar added.

"Oh no!" Ethan and Ella said at the same time.

"We weren't bored at all," Ella added.

"Good. Well, I'm afraid it's too late for our math lesson. We'll have to postpone it until tomorrow," Mr. Briar told the twins. "Your mom and I had a great idea, though. Why don't we go for your very first gondola ride? We know you kids were excited about that."

Ethan and Ella smiled at each other. It would be their *second* very first gondola ride in Venice!

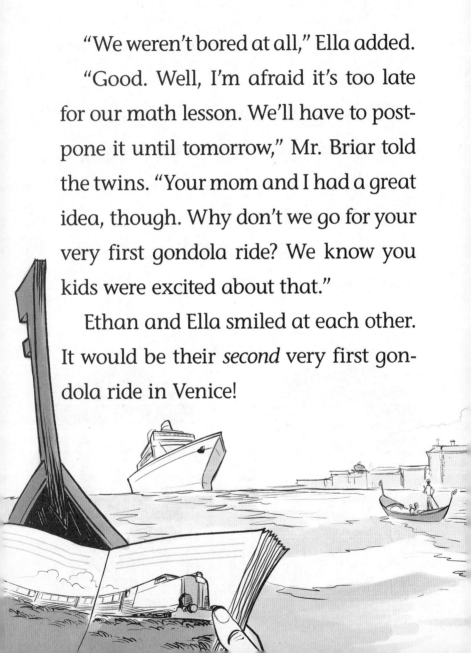

GREETINGS FROM SOMEWHERE

The Mystery of the Stolen Painting

#3

TABLE OF CONTENTS

CHAPTER 1

The City of Light

Ella Briar gazed out the airplane window. Down below, miles of glittering lights twinkled against the evening sky. "Look, Ethan!" she said to her twin brother.

"That must be Paris," Ethan replied. "It's awesome!"

"I think that's the Eiffel Tower," Ella said, pointing.

"Did you know that the Eiffel Tower is the tallest structure in Paris?" their dad, Andrew, called out from across the aisle. "It was built in 1889 for the world's fair."

"I see a river!" Ethan announced.

"That is probably the Seine," Mr. Briar guessed. "It divides Paris into two parts: the Right Bank and the Left Bank."

"We are staying in a lovely old neighborhood on the Right Bank,"

their mom, Josephine, said as she smoothed on lipstick. "There are a lot of fun shops there! *And* we'll be close to a famous museum called the Louvre."

Fun shops? A famous museum? The twins couldn't wait!

A short while later, their plane landed at the airport. The Briars took a taxi to the apartment they were renting. The building had no elevator, so they had to carry their suitcases up five flights of marble stairs. They were out of breath by the time they got to the top.

The climb was worth it, though. The apartment was enormous, with an elegant balcony that overlooked red rooftops and bustling cafés. Brightly lit boats cruised along the river. In the distance, the Eiffel Tower shimmered like a gold jewel.

Ella remembered from her dad's guidebook that Paris was often called the City of Light. Now she knew why!

Ethan ran straight to the biggest bedroom. "Dibs!" he shouted.

"Hey, not fair!" Ella protested.

"How about your father and I take this room?" Mrs. Briar suggested. "Ethan, there's a green room down the hall with soccer posters. And, Ella, the purple room has lots of books in English."

Ella loved books, and purple was her favorite color! She raced down the hallway with her suitcase and found her room. It had a canopy bed with a lavender bedspread. Black-and-white photographs of Paris covered the walls.

Next to the bed was a wooden bookshelf. Ella spotted a couple of books she'd already read, *Mrs. Frisby and the Rats of Nimh* and *Shiloh*. Tucked between them was a dusty old volume called *Les Secrets de Paris*.

Curious, she picked it up and flipped to the first page. It was all in French. However, someone had scribbled something in pencil. It was in English:

Paris is full of secret places that you will not find in any guidebook.

Ella shivered with excitement. What did that mean? Would she and Ethan stumble upon any of these secret places while *they* were in Paris?

CHAPTER 2

Strolling Through Paris

The next morning, the Briars headed out for a walk through the cobble-stoned streets of Paris. First, they stopped at a neighborhood café for a quick breakfast. The twins loved the fresh orange juice and croissants, which were flaky rolls shaped like half-moons.

After breakfast, they went to several shops to buy supplies for their picnic

lunch. They were going to have lunch at a park called the Luxembourg Gardens. They went to a *boulangerie* for bread. They went to a *fromagerie* for cheese. And finally, they went to a *pâtisserie* for pastries. Mrs. Briar put everything in a picnic basket she had found in their apartment.

"I've already planned a nice, winding route for us," Mr. Briar announced, holding up a crinkled map of Paris. "Oops. That's upside down. Here we go. Follow me, kids!"

Mr. Briar led the way. Mrs. Briar lagged behind as she took photos of the scenery and spoke into a tiny tape recorder.

Mrs. Briar was a travel writer. She and the family traveled to different foreign cities so she could write about it for her newspaper column, Journeys with Jo! While she worked, Mr. Briar took care of the twins and homeschooled them.

In the beginning, Ethan and Ella had not been happy about leaving Brookeston. They missed their house, their friends, their school, their second-grade teacher, Mrs. Applebaum, and most of all, their Grandpa Harry.

Still, their first stop—Venice, Italy—had been a lot of fun. The twins had even solved a mystery when a gondola went missing. And they really liked what they'd seen of Paris so far.

They crossed a short bridge and saw an enormous stone church.

"Kids, this is the Notre-Dame Cathedral," Mr. Briar explained. "See those statues up there that look like goblins with wings? They're called gargoyles, and they were put there as protection against evil." Mr. Briar was a history professor and knew lots of interesting facts.

Near Notre-Dame was a street full of tiny shops. A sweet, buttery smell was coming from one of them. "What's that yummy smell?" Ethan wondered out loud.

"That's a *crêperie*, or crepe shop. Crepes are thin pancakes with delicious ingredients rolled up inside, like chocolate and strawberries or ham and cheese," Mr. Briar replied.

"Can we get one? Can we get one?" Ella begged.

Mr. Briar laughed. "Maybe later. We don't want to spoil our appetites before our picnic!"

Soon, the family crossed back over the Seine on another, longer bridge. After a few blocks, they found themselves near a building that seemed to go on forever.

"Oh! This is the famous museum I mentioned last night—the Louvre!" Mrs. Briar said, snapping a picture. "Isn't it wonderful?"

"It used to be a fortress before it was a museum," Mr. Briar added.

Ethan could totally imagine soldiers inside, watching and waiting for enemy ships on the river. "Can we go in and look around?" he asked.

"They're closed on Tuesdays. But I promise we'll come back tomorrow," Mr. Briar replied. "Hey! Postcards!"

He and Mrs. Briar walked over to a street stand that sold souvenirs. Ella went over to the stand next to it, which sold jewelry. Ethan joined his sister just as a line of police cars sped by, their sirens blaring noisily. The sirens in Paris sounded different from the sirens back home!

Ella picked up a sparkly bracelet. "This is really pretty," she said to the woman behind the stand. "Did you make it?"

The woman didn't reply at first. Glancing past the twins, she twirled her long red hair nervously. She wore a ring that looked like a coiled silver snake.

"No, *mademoiselle*. I did not make it. Please give it back!" She grabbed the bracelet out of Ella's hands.

"Ella! Ethan! We'd better move on if we want to get to the

Luxembourg Gardens by lunchtime,"
Mr. Briar interrupted. He held a bag
of postcards in his hand.

As they walked away, the woman
reached for her cell phone and dialed
a number. She said something in
French. Her voice sounded urgent.

"Well she's not very friendly," Ella
whispered to Ethan.

Ethan nodded. "I know! I hope she's
not here tomorrow when we come
back," he murmured.

HARRY AND LUCY, Age 20,
AT THE SORBONNE

A New Mystery

Back at their apartment, the twins decided to check their e-mail before their homeschooling lesson.

Four messages popped up on the laptop screen. The first two were from Hannah, Ella's best friend from back home. The third was from Ethan's best friend, Theo.

The last message was a note from

Grandpa Harry. How exciting!

Ella clicked on his e-mail. Ethan leaned over her shoulder as they read it together:

To: ethanella@eemail.com

From: gpaharry@eemail.com

Subject: Sweets for my sweets

Hello, my dears. *Bienvenue a Paris!* (That means "Welcome to Paris!")

I hope you are enjoying the City of Light! Speaking of light, the Eiffel Tower has a special light show every night. Make sure you catch it. It is magical.

Did you know that I asked your Grandma Lucy to marry me in Paris? I was studying at the university to be an archaeologist. I asked her while we were having crepes at a very special *crêperie* owned by my friends on Rue de Fleur. (*"Rue"* means "street" and *"Fleur"* means "flower.")

Perhaps you will get a chance to go to this crepe shop. But a warning: Its name and exact address are a secret. Also, you must give a password at the door. It is *"faucon."*

Good luck, my dears! When you find the *crêperie*, please tell Jean and Jacqueline that their old friend Harry Robinson says *bonjour*! (That means "hello.")

Love,

Grandpa Harry

"A secret crepe shop?!" Ella exclaimed. "We have to find it!"

"Yeah, but how? We don't know what it's called—or where it is," Ethan pointed out.

"We don't know *yet*." Ella reached for her bag. She pulled out her notebook, which was purple with a shiny gold spine.

"What are you doing?" Ethan asked.

"Writing down our clues, *of course*," Ella replied, rolling her eyes.

Grandpa Harry had given Ella the notebook before the Briars left on their big trip. He'd told her that she might use it for solving mysteries. He had also given Ethan a going-away present—a gold coin with a picture of a hawk on it.

Ella opened her notebook to a clean page and wrote:

Rue de Fleur
Password: Faucon

Then an idea came to her. "Follow me!" she told her brother.

Ella closed the laptop and ran down the hall to her room, clutching her notebook. Ethan ran after her. Once there, she got *Les Secrets de Paris* from her bookshelf. She found the page with the handwriting on it and

then showed it to Ethan.

"'Paris is full of secret places that you will not find in any guidebook,'" Ethan read out loud. "What does that mean?"

"I'm not sure. But maybe Grandpa Harry's secret crepe shop is in this book!" Ella suggested.

The twins hunched over the old book and went through it page by page. But it was all in French, and they couldn't understand it.

At the end of the book was a map of the city. Ethan scanned it quickly.

"Rue de Flandre—was that the street he mentioned?" he asked Ella.

Ella glanced at her notebook. "No. It was Rue de Fleur. F-L-E-U-R."

The twins continued scanning the map. After a moment, Ethan found

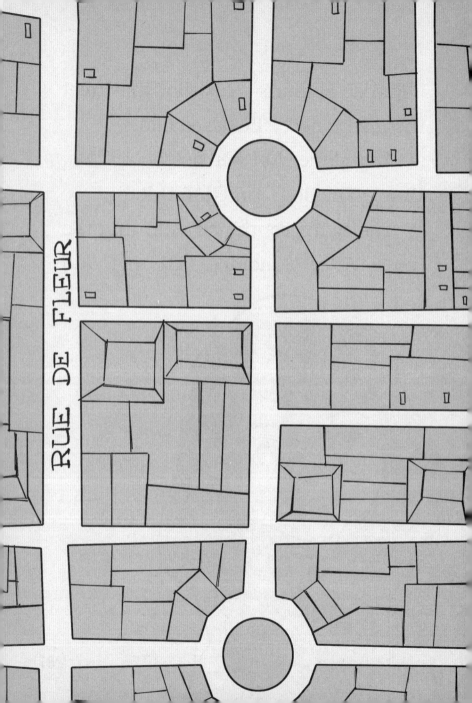

the street—Rue de Fleur!

"Here it is!" he practically shouted.

"It's near some big building called the Musée du Louvre," Ella noted. "That must be French for the Louvre Museum—"

"Where we're going tomorrow," Ethan said eagerly. "We can find the secret crepe shop then!"

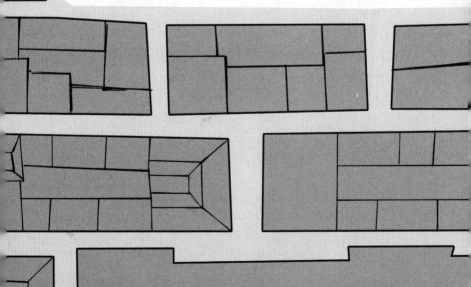

CHAPTER 4

Stolen!

The next morning Mr. Briar and the twins returned to the Louvre.

"The secret crepe shop must be somewhere near here," Ethan whispered to Ella as he looked around. "Now we just need to get away from Dad so we can find it."

Ella frowned suspiciously. "Get away from Dad? How are we going to do that?"

"We'll find a way," Ethan said with a sly smile.

The Briars entered the museum. There were so many things to look at! Ella's favorite was the marble statue of Nike, the Greek goddess of victory. Ethan loved the remains of the fortress

that used to be there. It was almost like going back in time to the Middle Ages!

After the fortress, they went to a crowded room that was filled with people. In the middle of the room was small portrait of a woman with long brown hair. There were mountains in the background.

"This is probably the most famous painting in this museum. It's called the *Mona Lisa*," Mr. Briar explained. "Do you know what's cool? No matter where you're standing, she always seems to be looking at you."

"No way!" Ethan said, surprised.

Curious, he walked ten steps to the left. The woman in the painting was still staring at him. He took ten more steps. She was *still* staring at him.

"Dad's right. You try it!" Ethan told Ella.

Ella repeated Ethan's steps. "That's

spooky!" she said after a moment. "Is the painting haunted?"

Mr. Briar chuckled. "I don't think so. Although there *is* a mystery surrounding the painting. Some experts think the *Mona Lisa* isn't who she appears to be, and—"

His words were drowned out by a loud alarm. A voice rang out over the speakers: "The museum is now closed. Please exit the museum."

Ethan glanced around. Everyone in the room was heading toward the doors. "What's going on?" he asked his dad.

"I'm not sure. It's probably just an electrical problem or something," Mr. Briar replied with a shrug. "Not to fear! I have more fun things planned for us after this!"

The twins followed their dad into the jam-packed hallway. As they neared the staircase, they overheard two women speaking in English.

"I just asked one of the museum guards. He said that an incredibly valuable painting has been stolen!" one of the women said.

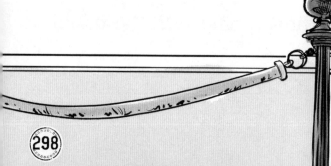

CHAPTER 5

The Thief
Leaves a Clue

"Ella? Did you hear what that woman said?" Ethan whispered.

Ella nodded. "Yes, a painting was stolen. That's awful!"

"I wonder if the thief is still here," Ethan said.

They glanced at their dad to see if he had heard, too. But he was busy reading his guidebook.

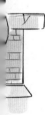

The three of them exited the museum. People had spilled out into the courtyard. A juggler entertained a crowd in front of one of the fountains.

Mr. Briar pulled his map out of his messenger bag. "Kids, I'm going to ask someone for directions to the Arc de Triomphe," he called out. "It's a monument that was built in honor of French soldiers. We can spend the rest of the morning there." He added, "Stay here. I'll be right back."

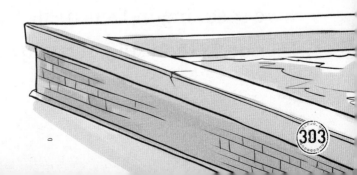

In the courtyard, a police offi-
cer was talking to a museum guard.
Ethan walked over to them.

"*Ethan!* What are you doing?" Ella
called out.

"I want to find out about the stolen
painting," Ethan replied. "Come on!"

Ella sighed and trailed after her
brother. When they got within ear-
shot, Ethan stopped and pretended
to tie his shoes. Ella pretended to get
something out of her bag.

But the police officers and the guard
were speaking in French. "It's no use.
Let's go," Ethan said, turning away.

Ella started to turn, too—then did a double take. The guard was showing the police officers a silver ring.

It was shaped like a coiled-up snake.

Ella frowned. The ring looked familiar. Where had she seen it before?

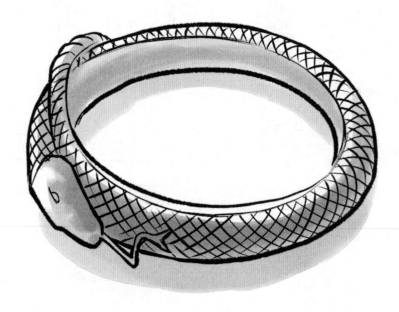

"The guard is telling the police officers that the thief left that ring behind," Ella overheard someone say.

"Kids, there you are!"

Mr. Briar rushed up. "You'll never believe it. I ran into my old friend Leo from college. He wants to have coffee at that café over there. Is that okay with you? We can go to the Arc de Triomphe afterward."

"Um, sure," Ella replied.

"No!" Ethan blurted out at the same time. "Ella and I really want to watch that juggler. Please?"

Ella stared at her brother. What was he up to now?

Mr. Briar pushed his glasses up on

his nose and checked out the juggler. "Hmm. He *is* very good! All right. I won't be long. Stay right here, and don't wander off."

"We won't!" Ethan promised.

As soon as Mr. Briar was gone, Ethan grabbed Ella's arm. "This is our

chance to find Grandpa Harry's secret crepe shop!" he told her.

Ella thought for a moment. "Okay," she said. "But first, there's something else I want to do. Can we go back to the jewelry stand from yesterday?"

"To look at more bracelets? No way!" Ethan complained.

Ella shook her head. "Not bracelets! I think I found a clue."

Ethan's hazel eyes widened. "What kind of clue?"

"The thief left a silver ring shaped like a snake," Ella explained. "The woman at the jewelry stand was wearing a ring like that. Remember? Maybe she's connected to the missing painting somehow!"

CHAPTER 6
A Speedy Getaway

A few minutes later, the twins found the row of street vendors from the day before. Tourists gathered around the stands, shopping for postcards and souvenirs.

Ethan and Ella spotted the red-haired woman right away. "There she is!" Ethan said excitedly.

The woman was talking on her cell

phone and putting all her jewelry into a black briefcase, as though she was closing up for the day. The twins moved closer, pretending to look at miniature Eiffel Towers at the next stand.

The woman spoke in French, so it was impossible to understand her. But at one point, she said something that sounded like: "Rue de Fleur."

"Did she just say 'Rue de Fleur'?" Ethan asked Ella. "Isn't that . . . ?"

Ella pulled her purple notebook out of her backpack and flipped through it quickly. "Yes! That's the very same

street Grandpa Harry's secret crepe shop is on!"

"We'd better talk to her right away," Ethan suggested. "Maybe she knows something about the missing painting *and* the secret crepe shop!"

But before the twins could question her, the woman took off down the street, clutching her briefcase. She jumped into a waiting car with tinted windows. The door slammed closed, and the car sped away.

"Oh no!" Ella cried. "Now what do we do?"

"I think we should try to find Rue de Fleur," Ethan said, watching the car weave in and out of traffic.

* * *

"We turn right here," Ella said, squinting at the map she had brought along. "Or is it left?"

Ethan leaned over to take a look. "I think we have to turn right when we get to this other street," he said, pointing.

The twins made it to the neighborhood where Rue de Fleur was supposed to be. But standing on a crowded corner, they weren't sure which way to go next.

"Where are the street signs?" Ella asked, glancing around.

Ethan frowned. His sister was right. Paris didn't have any street signs!

And then he noticed something interesting. The buildings at the corners of the intersection had small blue signs on the sides. The signs had fancy writing on them.

"That one says 'Rue de Rivoli,'" Ethan read. "*Those*

must be the street signs!"

Ella nodded. "Good! Let's follow those!"

The twins crisscrossed their way until they finally reached Rue de Fleur. It was a small street lined on either side by apartments and little stores, including several flower shops. Buckets of colorful blooms covered one section of the sidewalk.

"Yes! We found Rue de Fleur!" Ethan said excitedly. "Now all we have to do is find the secret crepe shop. And the jewelry lady, too."

Just then, a car with tinted windows

raced down the narrow street, its tires
squealing.

"Look out!" Ella shouted.

She and Ethan flattened themselves
against a building to avoid the speed-
ing car.

The car screeched to a stop and dropped off a passenger before driving away.

It was the red-haired woman!

CHAPTER 7
The Secret Crepe Shop

The red-haired woman rushed up to a brick apartment building. She had her briefcase with her. Using a key, she opened the front door and disappeared inside.

"Did she see us?" Ella asked Ethan nervously.

Ethan shook his head. "I don't think so. Let's follow her!"

"Follow her *where?*" Ella demanded.

"Just trust me," Ethan said.

He inched up to the first-floor window of the brick building. Ella followed close behind. The curtains on the windows were lacy and sheer, which made it easy to see in.

The twins pressed their faces to the glass—and gasped.

Inside the apartment, three people sat around a table, arguing in loud voices. One of them was the red-haired woman. The other two were men.

Propped up on the table was a beautiful painting framed in gold! It was a

portrait of a little girl with a dog.

Ella jabbed Ethan with her elbow. "That must be the stolen painting!" she whispered fiercely.

The red-haired woman opened her briefcase and spilled her jewelry onto the table.

Ethan gasped. "Maybe the bracelets and stuff are stolen, too," he said. "I bet she was trying to sell them at her stand!"

Suddenly, one of the men pushed back his chair, stood up, and started for the front door. For a split second, the twins watched in horror as the doorknob turned. They were about to be discovered!

"We have to hide. *Now!*" Ella cried.

She grabbed Ethan and pulled him away from the window. Glancing around frantically, she saw an open doorway one building over. "Quick! In here!"

The twins made a mad dash for the building and ducked inside. They slammed the door behind them.

"Phew, that was close," Ethan said breathlessly.

"*Bonjour?*"

The twins whirled around. A tiny woman with curly gray hair stood behind a counter. She peered at them

from over the top of her glasses.

"*Mot de passé, s'il vous plaît,*" the woman said with a stern expression.

The twins stared at each other.

"*Mot de passé,*" the woman repeated.

Just then, Ella noticed a familiar sweet, buttery smell.

Ethan seemed to notice it too.

"Crepes!" they said in unison. They had found Grandpa Harry's secret crepe shop!

"Oh! You are Americans?" The woman's expression relaxed into a smile. "I am sorry, I did not realize. Password, please."

"Get your notebook. Get your notebook," Ethan told Ella impatiently.

"I *know* that," Ella snapped. She reached into her backpack and pulled out her notebook. *"Faucon,"* she said to the

woman after a moment. "Did I pro-
nounce that right?"

"Yes, you pronounced it just
fine,'" the woman replied, still smiling at them. She pushed open a
door behind the counter
and waved them inside.
"Come this way, please."

CHAPTER 8

Heroes

On the other side of the door was one of the most wonderful sights the twins had ever seen!

It was a tiny room that was barely bigger than their tree house back in Brookeston. It had a few tables and chairs. A man stood at a stove, cooking a thin, golden pancake in a black skillet. He flipped the crepe over once,

twice—then put it on a plate. He sprinkled it with powdered sugar.

"Jean, we have customers," the woman announced to the man.

The man turned. He had bushy gray hair and a mustache, and he reminded Ethan of Grandpa Harry. "*Merci*, Jacqueline! *Bonjour, mes petits!* Hello, my children! What can I make for you today?" he asked in a merry voice.

"I . . . we . . . our grandfather sent us," Ella managed to say after a moment.

"Oh? Who is your *grand-père*?" Jean asked curiously.

"Harry Robinson. He said you were friends," Ethan piped up.

Jacqueline gasped. "You are Harry Robinson's grandchildren? We have not seen him in years! How *is* our dear friend Harry?"

"He's good. We miss him," Ella said timidly. "Oh, and he says hi," she remembered.

Jacqueline walked over to a wall covered with old photographs. She took one down. "This is a picture of Harry and Lucy when they were at the university," she said fondly.

The twins stared at the picture in amazement. Here they were across the world in a secret crepe shop, and it was as though Grandpa Harry were with them!

In the picture, he had thick black hair. Grandma Lucy had a long blond ponytail and looked a lot like their mom.

The picture in its pretty gold frame reminded Ethan of something. *Frame . . .*

"Painting!" he suddenly burst out. "We have to tell you about the painting!"

"What painting?" Jacqueline asked, confused.

"Some thieves stole a painting from the Louvre Museum this morning," Ella piped up. "They're hiding it next

door. We just saw it!"

"I heard about this on the news just now," Jean said, reaching for his phone. "We'd better call the police right away!"

* * *

Ethan, Ella, Jean, and Jacqueline watched from the window of the crepe shop as police cars pulled up in front of the brick building. A few minutes later, some police officers brought the red-haired woman and the two men out in handcuffs. Another police offi-cer carried the painting and jewelry.

"You are heroes!" Jean praised the twins. "Everyone in Paris will want to thank you for what you have done!"

Ethan shook his head quickly. "No. It has to be a secret! We're not even supposed to be here!"

Jacqueline looked at the twins, her eyebrows raised. "Oh?"

The twins explained about sneaking away from the Louvre while their dad had coffee with his college friend. "He'll be back any second now. We should go," Ella finished, looking at the clock nervously.

"But you can't leave until you've had some of my famous crepes!" Jean said, picking up his spatula.

Ethan glanced hopefully at Ella. She nodded.

"Yes, please!" they said in unison.

"Why do you keep your crepe shop a secret?" Ethan asked the couple.

Jacqueline wiped her hands on her apron and smiled as if remembering something. "Many years ago, Jean became known as the finest crepe maker in Paris. But he wasn't interested in becoming rich and famous. He just wanted to make crepes for friends and loyal customers."

"So we decided to start this little shop and give out the password to only a few people," Jean continued. "Our password has been the same for almost fifty years—*faucon*, or hawk." He added, "It's the same password that was used by a secret society that met here many years ago."

Hawk? Ethan reached into his pocket and pulled out the gold coin Grandpa Harry had given him as a going-away present. It had a picture of a hawk on one side.

Was it a coincidence?

Ethan was about to ask Jean and Jacqueline about their password. He also wanted to know more about the secret society.

But before Ethan could say anything, Jean held out two plates. *"Et voilà!* Here! Please eat these crepes while they are hot! These were your grandparents' favorites—lemon and powdered sugar."

The twins took the crepes and bit into them. They were warm and delicious and just the right combination

of sweet and tart. Ethan had thought croissants were his new favorite food. But now he knew it was definitely crepes!

"We really have to go," Ella said, nudging Ethan and pointing at the clock.

The twins finished up their crepes and said good-bye to Jean and Jacqueline.

"Please come see us again next time you are in

Paris," Jacqueline told them.

Ethan and Ella waved good-bye
and promised they would.

CHAPTER 9

The Eiffel Tower!

That night, Ella sat down at the laptop to send Grandpa Harry an e-mail. Ethan sat next to her, turning his gold coin over in his hand.

Dear Grandpa Harry,

Guess what? We found your secret crepe shop! Mr. Jean made us lemon and powdered sugar crepes. They were yummy.

Guess what else? We solved a mystery! Some thieves stole a painting from the Louvre Museum. We discovered them next door to the crepe shop. Mr. Jean called the police.

We learned that the secret password to the crepe shop is the French word for "hawk." Does it have anything to do with the hawk on the gold coin?

Tonight, Mom and Dad are taking us to the Eiffel Tower to see the light show you told us about!

We miss you! *Au revoir!* (That means "good-bye" in French!)

Love,

Ella and Ethan

Their parents came into the living room just then. Mr. Briar wore a T-shirt with the *Mona Lisa* on it. "Let's go to the Eiffel Tower!" he said eagerly. "Hey, I just heard some news on the radio. Did you know there was a big art theft at the Louvre Museum today? I guess that's why we had to leave. They caught the thieves with the help of an anonymous tip."

Ella blinked innocently. "Really?"

"Wow. We didn't know!" Ethan added with a grin.

Mrs. Briar patted her kids on their heads. "We should go. The light show will be starting very soon."

As they headed out the door, the twins exchanged high fives. They'd solved the mystery of the stolen painting and found Grandpa Harry's secret crepe shop all in one day. And now they were about to see a light show at the Eiffel Tower.

Could Paris get any better?

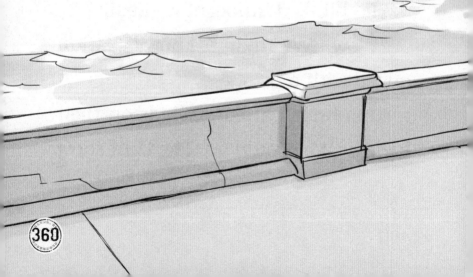

GREETINGS FROM SOMEWHERE

The Mystery in the Forbidden City

#4

TABLE OF CONTENTS

CHAPTER 1
Homesick in Beijing

"I miss Grandpa Harry's waffles," Ella Briar said with a pout.

"I miss the blueberry muffins from Petunia Bakery," her brother, Ethan, added.

The twins frowned at their plates, which were piled high with fried rice, pickled vegetables, and some foods they didn't recognize. The Briar

family was having breakfast at their hotel, the Beijing Imperial. The large dining room was decorated with red and gold furniture and paintings of swirly dragons.

"But, kids, we're having an eating adventure!" their dad, Andrew, said as he reached for his chopsticks. "Check out those delicious-looking *bao*!"

"Our neighbor Mrs. Chen used to make *bao* when I was growing up," their mom, Josephine, said with a smile. "My favorites were the ones with sweet beans in them. They tasted like little cakes!"

Ella picked up a *bao* and bit into it carefully. The steamed bun was warm and soft on the outside and filled with sweet barbecued meat inside. It was actually really good.

She still missed Grandpa Harry's waffles, though. He always decorated them with chocolate-chip smiley faces. Ella missed everything and everyone back in Brookeston. She knew Ethan did too.

The Briars had been traveling around the world for more than a month now. The reason for their big trip was Mrs. Briar's job. The *Brookeston Times* newspaper had hired her to write a travel column, Journeys with Jo!

They had already visited two cities in Europe: Venice, Italy, and Paris, France. After that, they had moved on to Shanghai, China. And just yesterday, they had arrived in Beijing, the capital of China.

"So what are we doing today?" Ethan asked. He stuck his chopsticks in his brown hair and made them stand up like antennas. Ella giggled. Her brother looked like a bug!

Mrs. Briar scrolled through her cell phone. "I just got an e-mail from my editor. He wants me to interview some people over at the National Art

Museum. I'm afraid I'll be tied up until dinnertime."

Ella's face fell. So did Ethan's. That was another thing they missed— spending time with their mom. She was always busy writing or doing research for her column. The twins were mostly with their dad, either sightseeing or having their homeschooling lessons.

Mrs. Briar reached across the table to squeeze their hands. "I'm sorry I can't be with you guys today. But guess what? The four of us are doing something really special tomorrow!"

Ella perked up. "What is it?"

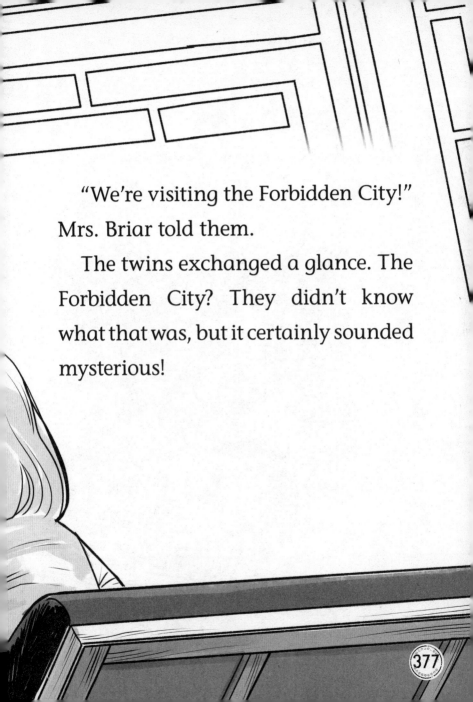

"We're visiting the Forbidden City!" Mrs. Briar told them.

The twins exchanged a glance. The Forbidden City? They didn't know what that was, but it certainly sounded mysterious!

CHAPTER 2

A New Mystery

That night in their hotel room, Ethan and Ella decided to check their e-mail before going to sleep. It was early for bedtime, but they were tired from spending the day working on math and science lessons with their dad. Second grade was hard!

The twins plopped down on Ethan's bed and placed the laptop between

them. Ethan wore his dinosaur pajamas. Ella's pajamas had hearts on them. Mr. and Mrs. Briar were in the next room, talking and drinking tea.

Ethan signed on to their account. There was an e-mail from Ethan's best friend, Theo. Theo had written that their soccer team, the Brookeston Boomers, had won their last match. There was another e-mail from Ella's best friend, Hannah, with a new poem for their poetry club.

There was a third e-mail, from Grandpa Harry. The twins opened it eagerly.

To: ethanella@eemail.com

From: gpaharry@eemail.com

Subject: The Three Dragons

Hello, my dears. *Huānyíng lai Beijing!* (That means "Welcome to Beijing!" in Mandarin.)

I hear that you are visiting the Forbidden City tomorrow. The Forbidden City was the emperor's palace for hundreds of years. It is called that because no one could enter or leave the palace grounds without the emperor's permission. (The word "forbidden" means "not allowed.")

These days, the Forbidden City is a tourist site. While you are there, be sure to go to the Imperial Garden. There you will find paths decorated with beautiful statues of animals. These statues are symbols for different things. (In Chinese culture, elephants symbolize strength; tigers symbolize courage; rabbits symbolize hope; grasshoppers symbolize wisdom, and so on.)

Perhaps you could look for the path that has my favorite statue. It's of three dragons. The dragons are red, green, and purple, and they symbolize good luck. In fact, I had some very good luck after I came across those dragons! Here is a clue: They are near the old pine tree.

Lots of love,

Grandpa Harry

Ella looked up at Ethan, her brown eyes twinkling. "A new mystery!" she exclaimed.

Ethan nodded. He and Ella loved solving mysteries. Back in Brookeston, they'd found Ethan's missing gold coin. It had been a going-away present from Grandpa Harry. In Venice, they'd tracked down a stolen gondola.

And in Paris, they had helped to catch a painting thief.

Ella reached across Ethan to grab something from the nightstand.

"Hey, you're squishing me!" Ethan complained.

"Sorry! I needed these." Ella held up her purple notebook and a pen.

"What for?" Ethan asked.

"To write down some notes about our new mystery!" Ella replied.

The notebook had been Ella's

going-away present from Grandpa Harry. Ethan watched as his sister wrote:

Go to the Imperial Garden in the Forbidden City.
Find the old pine tree.
Find the path with three dragons.
The dragons are red, green, and purple.

dragons = good luck
elephants = strength
tigers = courage
rabbits = hope
grasshoppers = wisdom

Ella closed the notebook and hugged it to her chest. "I can't wait for tomorrow!"

"Let's go to sleep! That way, tomorrow will happen faster," Ethan said with a grin.

CHAPTER 3

The Forbidden City

The next morning, the Briar family walked over to the Forbidden City. It was only a few blocks from their hotel.

Though she was still a little home-sick, Ella liked Beijing. It was both an old and a new city. Tall, modern sky-scrapers stood next to ancient temples. The streets bustled with cars, bicycles, and rickshaws, which were passenger carts drawn by bikes. Farmers sold fresh fruit on the sidewalks out of baskets that hung from bamboo poles.

Soon enough, the Briars reached the Forbidden City. It was surrounded by a moat. Ethan had read about moats in his books about ancient kingdoms. He never thought he'd see a real one, though!

"Let's play knights!" he suggested.

The twins pretended to ride on horseback across the moat bridge. They swung invisible swords through the air. Mr. Briar followed them with

his video camera while Mrs. Briar took photos.

The four of them made their way to the main entrance. After getting their tickets, they found themselves in a large square crowded with tourists.

Mr. Briar unfolded his pocket map and studied it. "The Hall of Supreme Harmony is straight ahead," he said, pointing. "I thought we could start there."

"Is harmony the thing we studied in music class?" Ethan asked.

"Yes, but in music, harmony means notes sounding good together. In this case, harmony means people getting along well together," Mr. Briar explained.

"Everything in the Forbidden City has a poetic name," Mrs. Briar remarked. "The Hall of Supreme Harmony . . . the Pavilion of Everlasting Spring . . ."

Ella repeated the names under her breath. They were so pretty! She wondered if she and Ethan should name their tree house

back in Brookeston. *The Tree House of Supreme Fun . . . The Tree House of Everlasting Snacks . . .*

Mr. Briar led the way through a gate that was guarded by two bronze lions. Just beyond was the Hall of Supreme

Harmony. It was an enormous building with red pillars and marble stairs.

Inside, a woman led a group of tourists. She was speaking English. Mrs. Briar went over and spoke to her.

"The tour guide said we could join her group!" Mrs. Briar explained when she came back. "This way, we can get

the true inside scoop on the Forbidden City."

"Sounds wonderful!" Mr. Briar said excitedly. He was a history professor, and he loved to learn about anything and everything.

Mrs. Briar slipped her sunglasses into her purse and turned to the twins.

"Stay close to us. Our guide said that there are more than nine hundred buildings in the Forbidden City—and more than eight thousand rooms."

Nine hundred buildings? Eight thousand rooms?

"Okay!" Ella promised.

Ethan nodded quickly.

"The Hall of Supreme Harmony is more than six hundred years old," the tour guide explained to the group as she led them into a large room. Colorful animal designs covered the fancy ceiling. "The emperor used to hold important meetings here. There were royal weddings, birthdays, and other celebrations here too. The last emperor of China was named Puyi," the tour guide went on. "He became the emperor when he was just two years old."

Ethan blinked. A two-year-old emperor? How was that even possible?

Just then, someone bumped up against Ella, which made her drop her bag. She bent down to get it—and noticed something odd. The man in front of her had a piece of paper stuck to his shoe.

Ella pointed it out to Ethan. "Maybe it's toilet paper!" Ethan whispered. The twins giggled quietly.

As the man moved away, the paper fluttered loose. But it wasn't toilet paper. It almost looked like a map!

Ella picked it up. It *was* a map. It was yellow and crinkly and looked old. There were strange symbols on it.

"Is it a map of Beijing?" Ethan asked.

"I don't know. It's not like the one Dad got from the hotel." Ella studied the map more closely. "This looks like a gate with two lions. Didn't we go through a gate like that?"

"Yeah, we did! Maybe it's a map of the Forbidden City?" Ethan guessed.

The twins tried to make out the other symbols. The room suddenly seemed quiet.

Ethan and Ella glanced up. Their tour group was gone. And so were their parents!

CHAPTER 4

Lost!

"Where did they go?" Ella cried out.

Ethan did a three-sixty spin, which was one of his favorite soccer moves. It allowed him to scan the whole room very quickly.

There were four doors leading out. Each door was decorated with identical designs.

Ethan pointed to the closest one

and said, "Let's try that way!"

"Okay," Ella agreed. She tucked the map carefully into her messenger bag, and the twins hurried to the door.

On the other side was a small room full of statues, sculptures, and paintings. A couple admired a bronze tortoise.

"Excuse me! Did you see our tour

group?" Ella asked them breathlessly. "Our mom and dad were with them. Our mother has blond hair. Our father is really tall. He has brown hair and glasses."

The woman shook her head. The man said something in Chinese.

"I guess they don't speak English," Ethan said to Ella.

"Thank you, anyway," Ella told the couple. *"Xièxie!"*

The man and woman smiled and nodded.

"Um, what did you just say to them?" Ethan asked Ella curiously.

"I said 'thank you' in Chinese," Ella replied.

"When did you learn Chinese?!" Ethan asked.

"Dad taught us

some phrases in Shanghai, remember? I guess you weren't paying attention," Ella teased.

"I was too!" Ethan snapped. Actually, he'd been sneaking peeks at his comic books during that lesson. "Come on. Let's keep going. We have to find Mom and Dad."

The twins went to the next room . . . and the next . . . and the next.

But there was no sign of their tour

group or their parents anywhere.

"Weren't we just here?" Ella asked when they reached yet another room.

"Were we?" Ethan glanced around. It was a small room full of statues, sculptures, and paintings. All the rooms looked alike!

"Now what?" Ella said, frustrated.

Ethan shrugged. "I'm not sure. How do you say 'we're lost' in Chinese?"

Ella reached into her bag and pulled out the crinkly old map. "I know! Let's use this map to find that garden Grandpa Harry told us about," she suggested. "He said the dragon path

there was good luck. Maybe we'll have some good luck, too, and find Mom and Dad afterward!"

"I like that plan. Does the map have any garden symbols on it?" Ethan asked.

Ella held the map up to the light. She and Ethan went over it carefully.

"What about this?" Ethan pointed to a symbol that looked like a tree. "Hey, wait a second. Didn't Grandpa Harry say something about a tree?" Ella got her purple notebook out of her bag. She opened it to the page about the Forbidden City.

"'Find the old pine tree,'" she read out loud. "'Find the path with three dragons.'"

Ethan's hazel eyes flashed. "That's it! The tree on this map is a symbol for the old pine tree in the Imperial Garden. If we can find it, then we'll find Grandpa Harry's dragons!"

The Gold Statues

After a few more wrong turns, the twins finally made their way out of the Hall of Supreme Harmony. They blinked in the sunlight and tried to figure out where they were.

They seemed to be in a courtyard. Pigeons fluttered and pecked at the ground. Tourists sat on stone benches or milled around a goldfish pond.

Mr. and Mrs. Briar were not among
them, though.

"I think we should go this way," Ethan said, pointing to a path.

Ella shook her head and pointed to a different path. "I think we should go *that* way. On our map, the skinny path leads to the tree symbol. My path is skinnier than your path."

Ethan shrugged.

They started down the path. They passed several more fancy buildings with red pillars. They also passed a bunch of tour groups. Ella spotted a man with brown hair and glasses in one of them. From a distance, he looked like Mr. Briar!

But when the man turned, Ella's hopes faded. Her dad was wearing his solar system T-shirt, not a shirt with a lion on it.

The twins continued walking. Gradually, the path grew narrower and less crowded. Then it curved to the right. Up ahead was a tiny red house. It reminded Ella of an elf's cottage from a fairy tale.

"What *is* that place?" she wondered out loud.

Ethan strode up to the door and

jiggled the knob. "It's open," he announced. "Let's check it out!"

"Ethan, I don't think we should to go in!" Ella warned him.

"Why not?" Ethan asked.

"We're the only people here. Maybe this part of the Forbidden City is *still* forbidden," Ella said.

"It's fine. Just trust me." Ethan pushed open the door and strolled in.

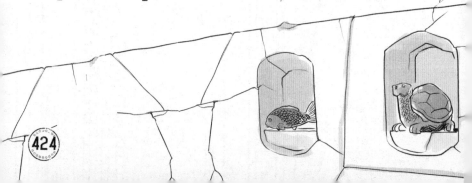

Sighing, Ella followed. She closed the door behind her.

The twins stopped—and stared.

The tiny red house had only one room inside. The room was no bigger than a closet and glowed with a shimmery light.

Hundreds of little gold statues were perched inside small holes that had been carved into the walls.

"This . . . is . . . so cool," Ethan said at last.

Just then, the door started to open. Someone was coming in!

CHAPTER 6

A Hopeful Surprise

Ethan froze as the door inched open.

He heard a woman's voice. She said something in Mandarin.

"Yes, we must find it!" another woman replied in English.

The twins held their breath. A second later, the door shut. The voices faded away.

"Whew! That was close!" Ethan murmured.

"Too close. We should go. I really don't think we're allowed to be here," Ella said nervously.

"Let's wait until those other people are totally gone," Ethan suggested.

"Okay. But if they come back and we get into trouble, it's your fault!" Ella told him.

Ethan shrugged and turned his attention back to the little gold statues. He recognized tigers, rabbits, and turtles among them.

"Didn't Grandpa Harry say that animals are symbols for different things?" he asked Ella.

Ella nodded. She flipped to the page in her notebook.

"'Dragons equal good luck. Elephants equal strength. Tigers equal courage. Rabbits equal hope.' And

'grasshoppers equal wisdom,'" she read out loud.

Ethan noticed a whole row of bird statues. One of the birds looked like a hawk. He dug through his pockets for the gold coin that Grandpa Harry had given him. The coin had an image of a hawk on it.

"Hey, Ella? Didn't we learn something about hawks in Venice?" he asked.

"Hmm, that does sound familiar." Ella turned to the beginning of her notebook. "Here it is! 'Hawks are messengers of the sky. They also symbolize nobility,'" she read. "If you're noble, that means you come from a very important and powerful family," she added.

"Well, the emperor's family is pretty important and powerful," Ethan said.

"Speaking of families . . ." Ella pressed her ear against the door. "We should keep looking for Mom and Dad. I don't hear those people anymore."

The twins exited the tiny red house. There was no one on the path except for a brown rabbit. It twitched its nose at Ella and Ethan and hopped away into the bushes.

Ella's face lit up. "Hey! Rabbits equal hope!"

"Well, then . . . I *hope* we get to the Imperial Garden soon. I *hope* the dragons give us lots of good luck. And I *hope* Mom and Dad aren't supermad at us," Ethan said.

The rabbit hopped to a tall red gate and disappeared through an opening.

Curious, the twins followed it through the gate.

On the other side was a beautiful

park. Flowers bloomed everywhere. There were temples and pavilions, too.

"Hey, this looks like the Imperial Garden!" Ethan exclaimed.

The twins exchanged high fives.

CHAPTER 7

The Dragons

Ella and Ethan were excited to find the Imperial Garden at last. Now all they had to do was find the old pine tree . . . and the path with the dragons . . . and, most important, their parents!

Ethan spotted a tour group standing outside a small temple. The tour guide was holding a little British flag. *Maybe he speaks English*, Ethan thought.

"Follow me," Ethan told Ella.

"Where?"

"That tour guide. He might be able to help us!"

They rushed over to the group. "Only the emperor and his family were allowed to spend time in the Imperial

Garden," the tour guide was saying. "They sipped tea, played chess, and practiced meditation on these grounds."

The tour guide paused to take questions from the group. Ethan raised his hand. "Excuse me! Is there an old pine tree near here?" he asked.

"Do you mean the four-hundred-year-old pine tree? Just follow this path until you get to a red building called the Hall of Imperial Peace," the tour guide explained. "The tree is right in front. It is known as the Consort Pine, and it symbolizes harmony between the emperor and empress," he added.

The twins thanked the guide and

hurried away. They soon reached the path.

"Look!" Ella cried out.

The path was decorated with stat-ues of different kinds of animals. They were exactly as Grandpa Harry had described!

Ella admired a sculpture of fish swimming in blue waves. It reminded her of the glass mosaic that she and Ethan had found in Venice. Ethan liked the statue of the galloping horses best. There were other animals too.

Now all they had to do was find the three dragons.

A few minutes later, they came

upon the Hall of Imperial Peace.

There was the old pine tree!

Ella had expected it to be tall and straight, like the pine trees they had back home. Instead, the Consort Pine looked like two curvy trees twisting and joining together.

Ethan circled around it. "Here's the path with the dragons!" he announced gleefully.

He and Ella looked up at the sculpture. Three stone dragons—one red, one green, and one purple—breathed fire at one another. Their eyes glowed orange.

"Isn't this awesome?" Ethan said excitedly.

"It's *super*awesome," Ella agreed. "What happens next?"

"I guess we wait for the good luck to happen," Ethan replied.

The twins sat down on a nearby

bench. Five minutes passed. Then another five minutes.

Ella tipped her face to the sky. "Good luck, where are you?" she called out.

Puffy white clouds drifted by. Birds soared through the air.

But nothing happened. Good luck didn't rain down from above. Mr. and Mrs. Briar didn't suddenly appear.

Ella tried to hide her disappointment. "Maybe the dragons don't work anymore."

"Maybe." Ethan seemed pretty disappointed too.

The twins stood up. Ella pointed to

the crinkly old map. "I guess we should
head back to the Hall of Supreme Harmony," she said slowly. She didn't know
what else to do.

"*Qǐngwèn! Qǐngwèn!*"

Ella turned around. A woman
rushed up to them, yelling in Chinese.
The woman reached out to grab the
map from Ella's hands!

CHAPTER 8

Found!

"Wait!" Ethan shouted as the woman reached for the map.

The woman hesitated. "Oh, you speak English?"

Ethan frowned. Why was the woman trying to steal the map asking them if they spoke English?

"My name is Li Mei. I work at the palace," the woman explained.

"Where did you get that map?"

"We . . . um . . . we found it in the Hall of Supreme Harmony," Ella admitted.

"It was stuck to a man's shoe," Ethan added.

"Oh, thank goodness!" Li Mei

cried out. "This is a very important ancient map of the Forbidden City. A famous archaeologist discovered it just recently."

"An important ancient map?" Ethan said, surprised.

"A famous archaeologist?" Ella said at the same time.

Li Mei nodded. "Yes. There is a special ceremony for it this afternoon. After the ceremony, the map is going into a display in one of our palace museums."

The twins stared at each other and then at the map. They hadn't realized that it was so valuable!

"I wasn't paying attention this morning," Li Mei went on. "All of a sudden, I noticed that the map was

gone. I thought someone had stolen it. But it must have been carried off by the wind."

"I'm glad we found it, then!" Ella said. She handed Li Mei the map.

"Thank you so much! You are quite the detectives!" Li Mei said gratefully. "But are you here by yourselves?" she asked with a concerned look.

Ella shook her head. "We came here with our parents. Our mom's a travel writer. We were supposed to spend today in the Forbidden City as a family. Except . . ."

"We lost them," Ethan finished. "We've been searching for them everywhere."

"Oh dear. I am so sorry. What do they look like?" Li Mei asked.

Ella described her parents.

"Oh! I just saw them in the Palace of Tranquil Peace!" Li Mei said, nodding. "I remember your father's T-shirt," she said with a laugh.

"Can you take us there?" Ethan begged.

"Of course! It is the least I can do for my young detectives who saved the day!"

Li Mei led the twins out of the Imperial Garden. Along the way, they passed the tiny red house from before.

"Hey, Ella! It's the place with the cool gold statues!" Ethan said excitedly.

Ella glared at him.

"What?" Ethan asked, confused.

"We weren't supposed to go inside, remember?" Ella whispered.

"Oh!" Ethan felt his cheeks grow hot.

Li Mei smiled. She didn't seem mad at all. "Those little gold statues

belonged to a long-ago emperor. It was his private collection. That is why they are here instead of in one of palace museums," she explained.

"I have a private collection too!" Ella told Li Mei. "Except I collect shark teeth and seashells."

"How wonderful!" Li Mei said, beaming.

A few minutes later, the three of them reached the Palace of Tranquil Peace. Inside, they saw a big tour group coming out of one of the rooms.

The twins recognized their tour guide
from before.

And just behind the tour guide were
Mr. and Mrs. Briar!

CHAPTER 9

A Secret Revealed?

Ella and Ethan thanked Li Mei quickly and then slipped quietly to the back of the group.

"How much trouble do you think we're in?" Ethan asked Ella in a low voice.

"I don't know. Probably a *lot*," Ella said worriedly.

Mrs. Briar waved to them just then.

She and Mr. Briar joined them.

"Isn't this a fabulous tour?" Mrs. Briar gushed. "I took so many photos for my column!"

"I'm glad you guys made some new friends," Mr. Briar added.

The twins stared at each other. *Friends?*

Ella glanced around. She saw that they were standing next to a dozen school children in uniforms.

Mr. and Mrs. Briar must have thought the twins had been with the school children all along!

"The tour's almost over. You two must be tired and hungry," Mrs. Briar said.

Ethan grinned at Ella, who grinned back at him. They weren't in trouble after all!

The tour group moved outside. Li Mei stood in the courtyard. She waved to the Briars and rushed up to them.

Ella gulped. Was Li Mei going to

give away their secret to their parents?

"Hello!" Li Mei said to Mrs. Briar. "My name is Li Mei, and I work here at the palace. We are having a special ceremony later for a very old map that was recently discovered. I wanted to invite you and your family

to the ceremony. I heard that you are a travel writer, and I thought you might find the ceremony interesting."

"Oh!" Mrs. Briar looked pleased and surprised. "I didn't realize people here knew who I was. We'd love to come to the ceremony. Wouldn't we, gang?"

"Yes!" Ella, Ethan, and Mr. Briar said at the same time.

Li Mei winked at the twins.

CHAPTER 10

Some Good Luck, After All!

The Briars attended the ceremony that afternoon. A lot of important-looking people gave speeches. Tea with jasmine blossoms was served along with delicious almond cookies. The map the twins had found was displayed in a glass case.

"Well, that was great!" Mr. Briar said after the ceremony was over. They had stopped at a café before leaving the Forbidden City.

"It was very nice of Li Mei to invite us. I still can't believe she knew that I was a travel writer," Mrs. Briar added.

"Yeah," Ella said, nudging Ethan. Ethan nudged her back.

"We'd better get back to our hotel and rest up," Mr. Briar said. "We have a big day tomorrow. We're going to visit the Great Wall. It's more than five thousand miles long! Oh, and tonight for dinner, I thought we could try some fried scorpion."

Fried scorpion? The twins stared at each other in horror.

Li Mei came up to the Briars. "I almost forgot. Here are some souvenirs for your children, from the gift shop," she said, handing Ella and Ethan two white paper bags.

Ella opened her bag. Inside was a little gold statue of a rabbit. Ethan's bag contained a little gold statue of a bird.

"These are copies of statues that a long-ago emperor had in his private collection," Li Mei explained. She winked at the twins again.

"Thank you!" Ella and Ethan said in unison.

"Wow, you kids are pretty lucky!"
Mr. Briar remarked.

The twins smiled. Grandpa Harry
had been right after all. The dragons
had brought them a whole lot of luck!

(#1) GLOSSARY

God morgon (Swedish) = Good morning

Bon voyage (French) = Have a good trip

Arrivederci (Italian) = See you again

(#2) GLOSSARY

basilica = cathedral

Benvenuti = Welcome

Buon giorno = Good day

Buona sera = Good evening

calle = street

campanile = bell tower

cristalleria = glassware

Grazie = Thank you

pesca = peach
ristorante = restaurant
Sì = yes
Ti amo = I love you
Venezia = Venice
zucca = pumpkin

*All words are in Italian.

(#3) GLOSSARY

Au revoir = Good-bye

Bienvenue = Welcome

Bonjour = Hello

boulangerie = bakery

crêperie = crepe shop

faucon = hawk

fleur = flower

fromagerie = cheese shop

grand-père = grandfather

Les Secrets de Paris = The Secrets of Paris

Mademoiselle = Miss

Merci = Thank you
mes petits = my children
musée = museum
pâtisserie = cake shop
rue = street
S'il vous plaît = Please
Voilà = There is/There's why

*All words are in French.

(#4) GLOSSARY

Hānyíng = Welcome to
                Beijing
Qĭnwèn = Excuse me
Xièxie = Thank you

*All words are in Chinese

CHECK OUT THE NEXT

GREETINGS FROM

SOMEWHERE

ADVENTURE!

Squaaaawk!

Ethan Briar woke up to a strange noise and glanced around, confused. Where was he? This wasn't his room. The bed was covered with a gauzy gold canopy, not soccer-ball sheets. He didn't recognize the tree growing in the middle of the room . . . or the lantern by his bed either.

His gaze fell on the window. A giant bird perched on the sill opened its long, thin beak.

Squaaaawk!

Ethan let out a yell. He'd never seen such an enormous bird before—at least not up close!

"What's wrong?" Andrew Briar called out from the other bed. He fumbled around for his glasses.

"Dad! There's a pterodactyl in our window!" Ethan exclaimed.

Mr. Briar slipped on his glasses. "Wow, it's big! No wonder you thought it was from the age of the dinosaurs.

I'm guessing it might be a hammer-headed stork. Or a sacred ibis. Wait. Let me look."

Mr. Briar reached over to the tall pile of books on his nightstand. "Okay, here we go. *Birds of Africa.*"

Africa! Ethan nodded to himself, remembering. They were in a lodge in the Maasai Mara National Reserve,

which was in Kenya. They had arrived last night with Ethan's twin sister, Ella, and his mom, Josephine.

The Maasai Mara was the latest stop on their trip around the world. Mrs. Briar was a travel writer for the *Brookeston Times*, which was their newspaper back home. Her job was

to write articles about different interesting places like Venice, Italy; Paris,
France; and Beijing, China. This week,
she was planning to write about the
Maasai Mara, which was home to
tons of wild animals, such as giraffes,
zebras, gazelles, lions, and more!

The fun part was that Ethan and
Ella would get to tag along to observe

the animals. The *not*-fun part was that they would have to return to the lodge with their dad every afternoon for their homeschooling lessons.

"I believe our visitor might be a purple heron!" Mr. Briar said, flipping through his book. "Apparently they are very good hunters. Maybe this one is looking for its breakfast."

Ethan eyed the bird nervously. "There's nothing here for you to eat!" he told the bird.

"It says right here that there are approximately five hundred different

kinds of birds in the Maasai Mara. I wonder how many of them we'll see on our safari," Mr. Briar said.

Ethan glanced at the window again. The bird looked at him and then flew away. Outside, the grassy brown savanna seemed to stretch on forever. There were only a few trees. The dawn sky was a mix of pinks and oranges and yellows. Ethan got back into bed.

Just then, there was *another* noise— this time, out in the hallway.

Knock. Knock. Knock.

Then the door burst open.

* * *

"Rise and shine, my friends!"

The Briars' guide, Kafil, stood in the doorway. He wore a khaki shirt, matching shorts, and hiking boots. A pair of binoculars dangled from his neck.

"Well, good morning, Kafil! What adventures do you have in store for us today?" Mr. Briar asked brightly.

"We have many adventures to look forward to, but only if we leave right away," Kafil said, tapping his watch.

"But it's six a.m.! Can't we go back to sleep for a bit?" Ethan complained.

"Not if you want to see the animals. They like to be out and about in the early morning because it is still cool out. Later, when it gets hot, they like to hide in the shade and take their naps," Kafil explained.

Ethan groaned. At this rate, *he* would need a nap later too!

Kafil disappeared down the hall to help Mrs. Briar pack up their things. Mr. Briar got ready and went to join them.

Ethan had just finished getting dressed when Ella skipped into the room. She carried their dad's laptop computer under her arm.

"You are soooo slow. I've been up for a whole hour!" Ella bragged.

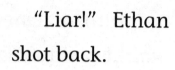

"Liar!" Ethan shot back.

"It's true. I got dressed, wrote in my journal, read two chapters of my book, and checked our e-mail."

"And?" Ethan asked.

"And we have a new message from Grandpa Harry!" Ella announced.

Ethan's face lit up. Grandpa Harry lived near their hometown, Brookeston. Before the Briars left on their big trip, they saw him all the time. Now they spoke to him only through e-mails and phone calls. The twins missed him a lot!

Ella put the computer down and opened up Grandpa Harry's message. She and Ethan leaned forward and read it together.

To: ethanella@eemail.com

From: gpharry@eemail.com

Subject: A lion sighting!

Hello, my dears. *Karibu Maasai Mara!* (That's Swahili for "Welcome to Maasai Mara.")

Did I ever tell you about my first safari in the Mara? Your grandma Lucy and I loved seeing all the animals. But we couldn't find any lions.

One night, we were on our way back to our lodge when our car broke down. We were frightened. Then, another car appeared. The driver was a scientist named Alex Broad. It turned out that Dr. Broad was studying the lions of the Mara.

Dr. Broad helped fix our car. The next day, Dr.

Broad invited us to go to a famous lake. During the long drive, we mentioned how much we wanted to see a lion. Dr. Broad stopped the car, got out, and imitated the cry of a wildebeest. A few minutes later, two lions appeared—a male and a female! Apparently, lions like to eat wildebeests. So we finally got our lion sighting. (And yes, we drove away quickly!)

I hope your safari is as exciting as ours was. And I hope you run across a lion or two (or more)!

Lots of love,

Grandpa Harry

"Now I really want to see a lion!" Ella said eagerly.

"Definitely," Ethan agreed. "But how?"

"Maybe Kafil will have some ideas," Ella suggested.

"I don't want to try Dr. Broad's wildebeest trick," Ethan said.

Ella shook her head. "Neither do I. I don't want to be a lion's dinner—or breakfast!"

The twins shivered.